# What Readers Are Saying

## TEXAS ROADS

*"Very good story with great characters and plot. A good lesson in following the path that you were meant to follow. I look forward to reading more of the Miller's Creek series."* ~Amazon Reviewer

*"Uplifting book, easy to read, engaging. Cathy Bryant is an excellent author. Her love and faith in God is evident in every word she writes."* ~Amazon Reviewer

## A PATH LESS TRAVELED

*"I 'stumbled' across this book for free in the e-book section. I know I 'found' it for a reason. If anyone is looking for the path to God, this is a very important book."* ~Amazon Reviewer

*"How often we miss God's perfect plan by following our own. Well written and so refreshing to read a great novel showing God's amazing grace and faithfulness."* ~Amazon Reviewer

## THE WAY OF GRACE

*"The Way Of Grace is a beautiful story of showing mercy and grace as Christ did. A few unexpected turns and keeps you wanting to read on. I Love this series of novels. Can't wait for the next one."* ~Amazon Reviewer

*"Cathy has done it again! Her books just keep getting better. With an air of mystery, this book grabs and holds the reader's attention from the start. Rather than just a*

'predictable' book, the story takes some unexpected twists and turns. It's not just a 'happily ever after' book; instead, the reader encounters a story of danger, courage, life-changing choices, love, and the amazing grace of God." ~Amazon Reviewer

## PILGRIMAGE OF PROMISE

"Though I have not read the earlier books in the series it did not take away at all from the story, which was engaging, humorous at times, and impeccably well done. Bryant has some really great talent and knowledge, something that is very obvious in her writing and characters. It was really hard to quit reading!" ~Amazon Reviewer

"For me, Pilgrimage of Promise was Karen Kingsbury meets Nicholas Sparks." ~Amazon Reviewer

## A BRIDGE UNBROKEN

"I am new to this series but A Bridge Unbroken grabbed me, pulled me in, and kept me hostage until I had finished. Cathy Bryant is so very good at taking her readers and immersing them into the story in such a way that you are emotionally involved. In a way it reminded me of L.M. Montgomery's ability to the same thing." ~Amazon Reviewer

"This book is another home run for Cathy Bryant! She has a shown a knack for writing books with a balance of romance, mystery, suspense and Christianity all in one book, or actually, into a series of books. There were times I was sitting on the edge of my seat in anticipation. I loved how I thought I had it figured out only to realize ~ not so much!" ~Amazon Reviewer

## CROSSROADS

"This is the best in the series so far--but I have thought that after every one!" ~Amazon Reviewer

"There are authors who write love stories full of cotton candy and ice cream sundaes, and then there are authors like Cathy Bryant, who write wonderful and beautiful stories of true love and life the way it actually is..." ~Amazon Reviewer

## THE FRAGRANCE OF CRUSHED VIOLETS

"I urge you, if you need to let go of something, no matter how big or small, take the time to read this book. Even if you think you are a forgiving person, like I thought I was, take the time to read this book. You won't regret it." ~Amazon Reviewer

"This was a very heart-felt book about forgiveness. It's about forgiving what is inexcusable. This caused me to pray and forgive decades-old grudges." ~Amazon Reviewer

## BELIEVE & KNOW

"My takeaway from this book is the importance of my responsibility to bring the knowledge of God to others. Believe & Know equips us to help...and be....'Truth-seekers.'" ~Amazon Reviewer

"Backed by Scripture and accompanied with thought provoking questions, this study will help you get grounded in the Word so you can talk to others about your own personal walk with God, the creator of the universe." ~Amazon Reviewer

## MILLER'S CREEK COLLECTION 1

"I have read all three books twice and would read them again. They each have a good story, easy to follow, well written. The characters are "real" people that I can identify with. I would recommend these books to anyone who loves a good story. I think what I like best is that they are written without any offensive language." ~Amazon Reviewer

"I love, love, love all of these books. They are well written, with characters that you will fall in love with. I laughed and cried throughout these books. You won't be able to put them down." ~Amazon Reviewer

## MILLER'S CREEK COLLECTION 2

"I have been a fan of Miller's Creek, the town, the people and the stories since I read the first book of the series. Born and raised in Texas, the people all seem like friends and neighbors I might have known. I love stories about kind hearted people whose lives are lived for the good of those they know." ~Amazon Reviewer

"This author is one of my favorite authors and I definitely recommend this set to anyone who enjoys excellent Christian romance." ~Amazon Reviewer

## MILLER'S CREEK FORGIVENESS COLLECTION

*"This is a wonderful book combination. The first book, A Bridge Unbroken, is a suspense and romance novel that had me hooked from the first pages. It is a story with lots of twists and turns that definitely kept me reading."* ~Amazon Reviewer

*"Excellent read on the topic of forgiveness. Well worth your time and money!"* ~Amazon Reviewer

# Pieces On Earth

a Christmas Novella

## CATHY BRYANT

WordVessel Press

# Books by Cathy Bryant

**Pieces on Earth**
© Cathy Bryant, 2015
**Published by WordVessel Press**
Santa Fe, New Mexico

To my three beautiful grandchildren. You are my legacy to the world. My heart's prayer is that you will come to know the One who made you and who loves you first and best. I also pray you will experience the perfect peace only He can give. Nana loves you always and forever.

*You will keep in perfect peace those whose minds are steadfast, because they trust in You.* ~Isaiah 26:3

# PART 1

*I heard the bells on Christmas day*
*Their old familiar carols play*
*And mild and sweet their songs repeat*
*Of peace on earth, goodwill to men.*

*One*

Liv finished filling out the necessary paperwork in the medical clinic waiting room, doing her best to keep her fears at bay.

She rose to her feet and carried the clipboard with the completed paperwork to the receptionist. The harried woman took the clipboard without so much as a glance her way. "Have a seat. A nurse will call you back momentarily."

Liv trudged back to the worn gray chairs and slumped into one of them, once more cognizant of her reason for being here. October marked her second month without her period. For most women her age, that would be a sign of promising things to come, but no such luck in her case. She'd known since her daughter's birth that having more children just wasn't in the cards for her. A fact that made Chesney's life even more miraculous.

She gnawed the inside of her lip and watched a little boy--probably about two years old--playing in the floor with a toy car. Without warning, the fear returned, bringing with it only one thought. Was it possible that she'd somehow inherited the gene that lead to the ovarian cancer that claimed her grandmother's life? Was that the reason for her current symptoms?

Liv pressed her lips together and forced her thoughts to happier ones. How wonderful it would be to add a fourth member to their clan. Chesney would make such a great big sister, and Jeff would be ecstatic to have another child. Since being promoted to lieutenant a few months ago, he had qualified for a stateside assignment as an instructor pilot at Pensacola NAS. How wonderful would it be to be able to raise a child with his or her parent actually around to help out? Even the few short months of having her daddy at home had made a huge difference in Chesney.

A pent-up sigh whooshed from her lungs. This current line of thought was landing her nowhere except in the dumps. There wouldn't be another baby. She grabbed her large sack of a purse and rummaged inside until she found an old envelope. Forcing the baby blues away, she started a to-do list of things to accomplish for her family's first Christmas together since before Chesney was born.

*Get the Christmas shopping done.* Well, that was a no-brainer. But this year it was especially important, since they'd also be buying gifts for nieces, nephews, siblings, aunts, and uncles. How fun it would be to have both sides of the family all together again in the mountain cabin vacation rental her mother had located online.

Now happy thoughts wound their way through her insides. Liv leaned her head back against the Plexiglas partition and allowed the happiness to wander unchecked.

Warm sweaters, cups of cocoa, a gigantic tree stuffed with presents, laughter of loved ones, and fluffy white snow.

Though she loved the sunny weather of Pensacola where Jeff was stationed, during the holidays she always yearned for the cold weather and snow of her Colorado upbringing. This year it would finally become a reality.

She straightened in her seat, checked the clock above the receptionist window, and returned to her list. *Buy Chesney some cold weather clothing.* Hmm, maybe she could order a ski bib online, since there was very little to no chance that she'd find one in Pensacola.

One thought led to another, and Liv scribbled as quickly as possible, unwilling to let even the smallest detail escape. A few minutes later, she brushed some escaped frizzy hair from her face and once more scanned her list. Yeah, that should do it. Now if she could just get these health concerns out of the way so she could concentrate on more pleasant tasks.

Liv glanced at the clock once more. Unbelievable. She'd been here for a half hour already. At this rate, she'd never make it to Chesney's preschool in time to pick her up. She grabbed her cell phone and hit speed dial for Darcy, one of many military wives in her group who all looked out for each other.

Her friend picked up immediately. "Hi Liv. What's up?"

"My blood pressure."

Darcy's contagious giggle sounded through the phone. "Let me guess. You're still waiting to see the doctor."

3

"How'd you guess?"

"Umm, 'cause I've been there and done that. Need me to pick up Ches?"

"Yeah, if you don't mind. And if a miracle occurs and I get out of here in time, I'll shoot you a text."

"Sounds good."

Liv had just dropped the phone back into her purse, when a short blond nurse in pink scrubs called her name from the doorway that lead to the exam rooms. She followed the nurse through the door where the dreaded scales awaited. After getting off the scales, fresh resolve took root in Liv's mind to cut back on carbs and lose those ten extra pounds that had plagued her since Chesney was born. Four years was way too long to lug around the unwanted weight. She followed the woman down the hallway and dutifully entered the room to which she motioned.

The nurse smiled and pulled the door toward the closed position. "Dr. Amy will be with you soon."

Liv perched on the edge of the exam table, once more on pins and needles about the potential problem. *Lord, please let me be okay, and please, please, please, don't let this affect our Christmas plans.*

The exam hadn't taken long, but Dr. Amy seemed preoccupied as she asked Liv question after question. In the end, the doctor had done nothing but order urine and blood tests. Now came the worst part. The waiting. Liv took a cleansing breath and wiped sweaty palms on her Capri pants.

As if on cue, the door opened, and the doctor entered, closing the door behind her. "Well, I think we have your diagnosis." Dr. Amy wore an enigmatic expression as she took a seat on a rolling stool in the exam room.

Liv swallowed to hopefully relieve her mouth of the immediate dryness. Was this news she was prepared to hear? And if her recent symptoms had to do with the "C" word that plagued her family, did she really want to know? She exhaled a quick puff of air through pursed lips. "Okay. And?"

A brilliant smile broke out on the middle-aged doctor's face. "You, my dear, are pregnant."

Her jaw dropped. "But how is that even possible? I thought--"

"According to your previous doctor's records, there was always the remote chance, Liv." Dr. Amy checked the file folder in her hands.

"I know, but the odds--"

"--were definitely not in your favor."

Liv allowed the news to truly sink in, and the smile Dr. Amy wore transferred to her own face. "I'm going to have another baby." The words came out in hushed wonder. Chesney and Jeff would both be thrilled, especially since they'd all given up hope of it ever happening. She ran fingers through her hair, partly to curb unruly strands, but mostly just to have something to do with her hands that had gone all flighty as soon as the doctor broke the news. "How far along am I?"

"Just a few weeks. For a due date, I'd say an Independence Day baby."

She gave her head a shake. This was the perfect gift for Jeff for their first Christmas together in several years. Already, a date with Pinterest loomed in her plans for the immediate future. There had to be a unique and Christmas-y way to pull off the baby announcement to both her husband and their families. "Wow. I'm still trying to wrap my head around this."

Dr. Amy laughed. "That's understandable, but I'm sure it will get real soon enough." The woman's face sobered a bit. "Not to worry you or anything, but with your medical history, you will need to be especially careful."

Liv nodded. That was to be expected. Chesney hadn't made it full term, but at least she'd made it long enough to survive, even if it had meant an extended hospital stay.

The doctor stood, opened the door, and faced Liv once more. "Be sure you stop by the front desk on your way out to schedule your next appointment. I'll see you in about a month."

A few minutes later, Liv stood outside in the beautiful Florida sunshine, her heart as free as the seagulls who cried out their typical sea breeze joy. One would never guess it was October by the balmy temperature. A fact that didn't bother her in the least. Because come December, she and Jeff and Chesney would be up high in the mountains of

Colorado, surrounded by their families and crystal white snow.

The years of struggling to make it through another Christmas alone entered her thoughts, but she forcefully shook her head. Not this year. And with Jeff now in a training position, hopefully never again.

Liv checked her watch. Just enough time to pick up Chesney from school, after she sent Darcy a quick text.

# Two

Once back at the house, Liv looked on as her daughter scaled the kitchen island bar stool and scooted around until she sat facing Liv in the kitchen.

Liv spread peanut butter on one half of the bread slice and grape jelly on the other half. "I've been meaning to ask you about the Bible stories Daddy's been telling you at bedtime. Do you like the new Bible story book Grandma Hope sent?" Liv smiled as she thought of her mother. Though generally quiet and retiring, as well as diminutive in stature, the woman's faith was larger than life. And when it came to her grandchildren knowing about God, she left no stone unturned. Her mom had rightfully earned the title of faith warrior for their families, determined that all of her grandkids would be with her in heaven some day. Liv folded the bread and slid the sandwich plate across the counter toward her daughter, waiting for an answer.

Chesney picked up the sandwich and took a big bite, nodding her head at the same time. "Yeah."

"What are the stories about?"

Speaking around bites of sandwich, her daughter answered. "Well, there was one about King Daniel."

"You mean King David."

Her daughter's face went blank, and she stopped chewing momentarily. "I thought David was the one in the fiery furnace."

"No, that would be Shadrach, Meshach, and Abednego."

"Oh, those three guys."

Liv couldn't help the smile that flitted to her lips.

"So those three guys were in the fiery furnace *and* the lion's den?" Chesney had her head cocked to one side, her dark red wavy hair dangling down.

Now Liv laughed outright. "No, Daniel was in the lion's den."

Chesney licked a blob of peanut butter and grape jelly from her fingers. "They all get tangled up in my head." She finished off the sandwich and chewed, once more talking around the food. "Can I go play in the backyard?"

"Yes, you may."

As she watched her daughter scuttle to the sliding glass doors and out into the sunny yard, Liv considered her daughter's words. Yes, it was good that Chesney understood the individual meaning from each story, but her daughter was missing the bigger picture. Liv skewed her lips to one side. Somehow she had to find a way--not to relay a bunch of unrelated stories--but to tie them all together for her young daughter, so she got a good grasp on the overall message of the good news of God. After all, knowing her mother, Grandma Hope would probably give each of her grandkids a pop quiz at Christmas.

Liv finished a quick clean-up of the kitchen, washed and dried her hands, and then checked to make sure Chesney was still in the backyard. Her daughter played happily in the sand box Jeff had built for her this past summer. Feeling free and lighthearted at all that had transpired that day, Liv snatched up her tablet and moved to the sofa to check out baby announcement ideas on Pinterest.

Later that night, after bath time, Liv approached Jeff, who sat at the dining room table reading the newspaper. She'd been especially carefully not to be too exuberant, or her detail-oriented husband would know in a heartbeat that something was up. "Jeff, if you don't mind, I think I'll switch things up with Chesney's bedtime story."

He looked up at her, a slight furrow between his dark eyebrows. "Was I not doing it right?"

Liv laughed. "You were doing it just fine, but I want to try an approach that will hopefully help her see the big picture of the Bible. You on board with that, sailor?"

A grin popped on her husband's face at the naval terminology. "Sure. Want me in there with you?"

"Always." She sent a teasing wink and headed down the hallway to their daughter's room, her ever-helpful hubby on her heels.

A few seconds later, they all lounged on Chesney's bed, leaned up against the frame, with their daughter cradled between them. Liv reached for the Bible she'd placed on the nightstand. "Time for a bedtime story."

Chesney looked up at her like she'd lost her mind. "That's a big story."

Jeff laughed out loud. "The biggest story of all time." He tickled Chesney under her chin until she giggled and ducked away from him.

Liv's heart immediately fluttered. He'd always been a great dad, in spite of his frequent tours of duty. *God, thank You for this new baby for all of us, but especially for Jeff.* Liv tried to speak in a normal voice. "And it's a story we're a part of." She smiled down at Chesney.

The statement had the intended effect. "We're in the story?" Chesney's eyebrows crinkled in a comical way.

"Yes. But the part I'm going to tell you tonight is about God and the very first man and woman."

Chesney's face brightened. "I know this story. Daddy told it to me not too long ago. God made the world and everything that was in it, then put Adam and Even in the garden of Even."

"You mean the garden of Eden?" Liv over-pronounced the "d" so Chesney would get it right.

"Oh, okay. That place."

Jeff leaned down near their daughter's face. "But do you know how God made the world?"

Chesney lifted wiggling fingers high in the air, her face overly dramatic. "Alacajamkazoo. And poof, there it was."

Liv giggled. "Well, not quite. All God had to do was say what He wanted and it happened. He said, 'Let there be light,' and there was light."

Their daughter's eyes were wide with wonder. "That's amazing. Is that how he created Adam and Eve, too?"

Jeff joined in. "No. The Bible says God stooped down and made Adam by shaping him out of the dirt."

The expression that landed on Chesney's face clearly revealed that she found that idea totally preposterous. "Like a mud pie?"

"No, silly." Liv opened her Bible to Genesis and read the passage directly from the Bible.

"And what about Eve? Did God make her out of dirt, too?"

"When God saw that Adam was lonely, he put Adam to sleep, took out one of his ribs, and created the woman." Jeff spoke the words reverently, then looked up at Liv with a gleam in his eyes. "Adam was very happy about having a helper."

Liv's stomach did a quick somersault. The good news she hid inside threatened to spill out on the spot. She caught a quick breath and captured her daughter's attention. "But what is really cool is that God made the garden first, and He included everything that Adam and Eve would need to live and be happy. He made it perfect just for them."

"So they could live happily ever after just like us." With those words, Chesney wiggled down under the covers and smiled up at her parents. "Good night, Adam and Eve."

All of them shared a laugh. and after good night kisses, both Liv and Jeff laughed all the way out of the room.

Her eyes a-twinkle, Liv handed the Bible to Jeff as he closed the door behind them. "Here you go, Adam. Put that away for me, will you?"

# *Three*

L ater that same week, Liv snatched one of Jeff's bright white t-shirts from the laundry basket and folded it. Just as she laid it on the stack of other t-shirts, the bedroom door opened and Jeff stepped inside, a beleaguered expression on his face. Liv reached into the basket for another piece of clean laundry. "You're home early. Everything okay?"

He didn't speak, but strode into the master bathroom and closed the door behind him. A second later, from within the bathroom, water spewed from the faucet. Then the faucet went silent and the door opened, the grim look still firmly implanted on her husband's face.

His expression brought on a moment of panic inside of Liv, but determined to not let her fears get the best of her, she took a cleansing breath and motioned to the bed beside her. "Okay, mister, park it, and tell me what's going on."

Jeff dropped his weight onto the bed, his upper lip pulled between his teeth and his gaze averted. Finally he released a heavy sigh. His lips clamped into a thin line, and his head shook from side to side, like he wasn't quite sure what to say. Or how to say it.

"You're officially starting to scare me, Jeff. Spill it."

He made eye contact, enough for her to see the storm in the hazel eyes that matched Chesney's. "You're not going to like it. I don't want to tell you."

Liv took a seat on the bed on the other side of the basket, her heart pounding so hard she could feel it in her temples. She closed her eyes, already trying to come to grips with the news he was about to deliver. "You're being deployed."

Jeff's silence was the only affirmation she needed.

The room grew deathly quiet, the air so thick it was palpable.

With shaky breaths and pinched lips, Liv did all she could to control the rising tide of white hot anger within. All their plans. Plans they'd made, assured that they could finally have a white Christmas together as a family. Then in a move that surprised even her, she hurled the laundry basket to the floor with a guttural scream. "You told me that being an instructor would keep this from happening."

"I thought it would. But the Navy needs some experienced pilots for an upcoming mission."

Tears now coursed, unchecked, down Liv's face. "When?"

"It's a quicker than normal turnaround."

"When?" She nailed him down with her angry gaze.

His Adam's apple bobbed briefly. "Next week." His gaze shifted downward. He released a measured breath between protruding lips, then met her angry glare once more. "They're telling us this one could be especially dangerous."

"Afghanistan again?" The words sounded as though from the deep recesses of her heart, dredging up all-too familiar fears.

Jeff swallowed hard and nodded.

Something inside broke. So much for their plans for a white Christmas in Colorado with their family. So much for her special surprise. So much for having Jeff home safe and sound, with no cause to worry about anything but how well the trainees accepted his instruction. With fisted hands, she swiped away tears that leaked from her eyes. "Well, you're just going to have to tell them no. We've already made plans for Christmas. We haven't had a Christmas together in years, and this one was supposed to be special, back in Colorado with our family."

His eyes held incredible sorrow. "Liv, you knew when you married me that--"

"Yes, but I thought it was different now." Liv cut him off with her poison-laced words. She'd thought that this year would be better. She raised both hands to her head, clutched handfuls of hair made more frizzy by the unrelenting humidity and closed her eyes against demons within. This was all more than she could handle at the moment. Propelled to action by the news that had ruined everything, Liv jumped to her feet and ran from the room, slamming the door behind her so hard that one of the wedding photographs hanging in the hallway crashed to the tile floor, where the frame and glass shattered into pieces.

With the ache in her heart also weighing down her shoulders and dispensing tears down her cheeks, Liv stooped to pick up the photo before the glass marred the portrait, overwhelmed by one thought. The broken frame was the perfect analogy for her life. One minute she'd been on top of the world, happily planning her family's white Christmas and life-changing announcement of a new baby. Then in the next moment, she knelt among nothing but the broken pieces of her now-shattered dreams.

The week preceding Jeff's departure flew way too quickly. In previous deployments they'd had several weeks to prepare, but because of the rush of this particular mission, everything had been crammed into one lousy and pain-ridden week. Physical exhaustion had become the standard mode of operation. In the midst of all the details of Jeff's deployment and trying to give Chesney as much time as possible with her daddy, Liv had tried to get over her hurt by shoving it deep inside. So far, that technique wasn't working especially well.

On the day of his departure, during her early morning time with God, everything felt forced, a matter of soldier-like routine and duty, rather than the intimate warmth and joy Liv had come to experience. To make matters worse, the sibilant hisses of another voice had taken up resident in her head. A voice that encouraged her to encase her heart in icy cold steel. A voice that held more sway at the moment than she cared to admit.

Liv closed her eyes against the frozen hardness in her heart. *Lord, help me get past this without falling apart. Again.* She crossed her arms and moved into the living room.

Jeff--clad in his classic blue-tone Navy fatigues and black boots--was minutes away from walking out the front door. Who knew how long it would be before they saw him again...if ever. She pushed the negative thought aside and stepped forward to give him a hug she didn't feel. It was like part of her had frozen over completely. Brief tears stung her eyes, but she quickly brought them under control and took a step back. "Keep us informed as much as possible."

Jeff's face registered profound hurt at her coolness. "You know I will." He hesitated and then cocked his head slightly to the right, his eyes pleading. "Liv, please don't let this come between us. It doesn't have to be this way. I need to know you and I are okay before I leave and face whatever lies ahead."

While his words were true, they were also false. "I understand what you're saying, Jeff. Really I do. And I want to be there for you, but I can't pretend something I don't feel. This is just going to take some time for me to process." Would she ever be able to forgive the Navy and Jeff? And even God? Then, at the last possible minute, her prior deployment experience kicked in. She hugged him once more. "I love you, Jeff. Please come home to us safe and sound." Should she tell him about the baby? Would that make it easier or harder for him to leave?

"Daddy!" Chesney yelled from around the corner and down the hall, followed by the hollow slam of her bedroom door. She rounded the corner, a paper clutched to her chest. She flung herself into Jeff's outstretched arms. "I made you something." She held the paper toward him.

"You did?" He perused the paper, his eyes brightening with tears.

"It says 'I love you' and 'be careful.' Mommy wrote the words out so I could copy them."

He hugged her neck, smiling his appreciation and love to Liv. "I see that. Thank you, baby girl."

A minute later, he set Chesney's feet on the floor and knelt beside her. "You be a good girl for your Mommy, okay?"

Chesney nodded, her eyes already bright with unshed tears. Even at the tender age of four, Chesney had unfortunately learned about the goodbyes that came with having a father in the military. Already she had taken on the stoicism of someone far older.

Jeff stood and pulled Liv into another embrace. "I love you, Liv, and I always will." He whispered the words against her hair, his lips briefly brushing against her ear.

A lump formed in her throat. She battled to find the strength to give him the words of encouragement she knew he sorely needed, but no words would sound.

He released her, sent her one last pleading look, then walked out the door without so much as a second glance.

With the familiar cold freezing her veins to solid ice, Liv quietly shut the door and leaned against it as her sobbing four-year-old crumpled to the floor in utter heartbreak.

# PART 2

*And in despair I bowed my head*
*There is no peace on earth I said*
*For hate is strong and mocks the song*
*Of peace on earth, goodwill to men.*

# *Four*

"Liv, I know this is hard. You know I've been where you are."

Liv curved an arm around her waist as she held the cell phone to her ear. Yes, her mother had endured a lifetime of military service being married to her Air Force dad. Military service that would never be awarded with a medal or recognition of service rendered.

"I know Mom, but this time it's somehow different." Because of the baby? And how was all this stress affecting their unborn child? "I'm trying to get over it, but I just can't."

"Then you're just not trying hard enough." Mom's voice took on the stern quality of a woman in charge, the same voice she'd used during Liv's growing up years while Dad had been shuttled away for months at a time by the Air Force.

Liv struggled to find words, but none came. Not a day went by that she didn't long for her husband to be at home with them. That alone ate up enough energy to make trying to get over it even possible. She longed to tell her mother about the baby, but just couldn't. Not at this point. It was too soon. Her pain still too raw. Yet even in the knowledge that she wasn't ready came the startling realization for potential destruction unless she got a firm grip on her anger and resentment. Somehow she had to find a way to get past this. To forgive all parties. She rubbed straightened fingers resembling a mock salute against her furrowed forehead.

"Honey, you've just got to let it go. If you don't the hopelessness will literally eat you alive. Trust me. I know." Mom paused momentarily, as if waiting for a response. When she got none, she continued. "You have to depend on God."

Easy to say, not so easy to do. Besides, she had depended on God. Had prayed for this holiday with her husband. And look where it had gotten her.

"Satan wants to keep you where you're at. Don't give him an inch, or he'll take a mile. I promise you that."

The truth of her mother's words echoed in her hollowed-out heart. Yes, the enemy wanted to keep her in pieces rather than experiencing God's peace. "Okay, Mom. I'll try." The words barely sounded, and with absolutely no conviction behind them.

"It would also help if you found something to occupy your time while Chesney is at school."

Liv nodded. "Actually I've started taking photographs to hopefully sell online." She opted not to tell her mother about the pottery lessons that had been arranged.

"Glad to hear it." The phone grew silent for just a moment, then Mom started in again. Good thing that at least one of them was able to carry the conversation. "Are you and Chesney still coming for Christmas?"

Good question. "We're gonna try." Airline tickets were too cost prohibitive and out of the question. Could she make the grueling 1400-mile drive on her own with a four-year-old in tow? Would it be too much for the baby? A sudden resolve straightened her spine. She could and would do this. "You know what? We'll be there. And we might come early and stay late." Jeff's absence carried with it the unexpected bonus of no timeline. Yes, Chesney might have to miss some school, but it was a minor issue at her age.

"That's my girl. I knew you'd bounce back from this."

Liv's mouth flat-lined. If the truth were known, she hadn't bounced back at all. Instead her plans to make the trip on her own had come from a place of sheer fear, hurt, and anger. A place she grew more and more familiar with by each passing day.

Liv pulled her knees to her chest later that evening, leaned against the headboard of Chesney's bed, and looked down at her daughter. So far the idea to tell Bible stories to Chesney in the context of the bigger story was working, even in spite of the fact that she didn't tell pieces of the story every night. Instead she'd made the conscientious decision to tell a little at a time, allowing room for discussion in between.

Liv pressed her lips together. Unfortunately, tonight's part of the story held implications for her own life.

Implications she didn't particularly want to acknowledge or deal with. "Adam and Eve didn't mean to mess up their perfect world, but it happened because they believed the lie the snake told them." The truth of the words in relation to her current circumstances tugged at her heart, but she ignored them and honed in on what her daughter was saying instead.

"Sorta like me at school."

"What do you mean?"

Chesney wrinkled her nose as if remembering something distasteful. "At recess, A.J. told me that Miss Cindy told him to tell me that I needed to go pick up the trash on the big kid's playground, and that I could play on their swing set while I was there."

"And you believed him?"

Chesney's red wavy curls jiggled as she nodded her head up and down. "Yeah."

"So what happened?"

"I went and picked up the trash. Then I played on their swings. After that I went down the big slide."

"And?"

Her daughter brought fingers up to scratch an itch on her cheek. "Miss Cindy came over and griped at me for breaking the rules." Her daughter's expression grew doleful. "It made me sad that Miss Cindy was mad at me. I thought she didn't like me any more. And it was all A.J.'s fault."

The perfect analogy for this part of the Adam and Eve story, as well as the brokenness in her marriage at the moment. "Well, not exactly. You could have gone and asked Miss Cindy if what A.J. said was true. Sounds to me like you believed him because you wanted to play on the other playground. Am I right?"

Chesney nodded somewhat dolefully.

"Something similar happened to Adam and Eve. God gave them the rule not to eat from the one tree, but the snake lied to them and told them it was okay. That they would be like God if they did. But once they ate the fruit of that tree, they were broken."

"Broken in pieces?"

"Sort of. Just like with you and Miss Cindy, Adam and Eve's relationship with God was broken. See, God is perfect and holy, and because Adam and Eve believed the lie and acted on it, now they were unholy. Though their bodies didn't get broken right away, their lives were. They had to leave the garden."

"Forever and ever and ever?"

Liv nodded.

"That makes me very sad. Did God gripe at Adam and Eve the way Miss Cindy griped at me?"

The curses God pronounced on them floated effortlessly to the front of Liv's mind. "Sort of. He told them that the earth would be a more difficult place to live in because of their bad choice."

Her daughter's face took on a solemnity beyond her years, and her forehead wrinkled into a dark frown.

Liv tweaked her daughter's pug nose. "But God also made them a promise."

"What promise?"

"He told them that one day a Fixer would come who would fix them and get rid of the snake and all his lies."

Chesney's face brightened. "Yay, God!"

A laugh bubbled up inside of Liv, the first one she'd had in days. Yay, indeed. Now if she could only bring about the changes she needed to make in her own broken life. The thought brought nothing but questions. Just how was she supposed to do that? And did she really want to expend the effort to bring it about?

# Five

"Sorry, Darcy. Chesney and I can't go to church with you tomorrow. We have other plans." The lie rolled effortlessly from Liv's lips. Once she made it past the momentary stab of regret, the next lie was much easier. Hadn't the same thing happened in her last e-mail correspondence with Jeff?

Her husband had also asked how things were at church. Rather than confess that she hadn't been attending services, she'd simply told him things were fine. But things weren't fine, and she knew it. Not only had they stayed away from church, but her efforts to pray and read her Bible each morning had more and more been falling by the wayside.

"Well, we sure do miss you. Are you certain you're okay?" Her friend's voice held genuine concern.

"We're holding our own." Were they really? The sharp shards of broken pieces still pierced her heart, with bad dreams and nightmares replacing God's peace as her mind focused in on the potential for disaster and devastation in the messed-up world in which they lived.

"Okay, then." Darcy's tentative voice revealed that she in no shape, form, or fashion believed a word. "How about getting together on Tuesday for a lunch date?"

"Can't." The word pounced out like a stalking cat, sharp claws exposed. "Debbie and I are going shopping." Another commonplace activity. So much so that after only a few weeks of life without Jeff, the credit card bills were mounting. But she had to have some way to cope, right?

"I'm glad you and Debbie have hit it off. She needs you as a friend."

Liv's thought turned to the always-fashionable Debbie. Surely if anyone had it all together, it was her. Never had she met someone so self-assured and comfortable in her own skin. Liv sighed. Both things she sorely wanted in her own life. Darcy had it all backwards. "I guess we need each other."

No response sounded on Darcy's end, so Liv brought an end to the call. As she said goodbye to Darcy and laid down her phone, a sudden guilt-laden thought pelted Liv's mind. Darcy had always been there for her, had been a true friend in the worst of times. But now, for whatever reason, their interactions left Liv annoyed and uncomfortable. So uncomfortable that from deep inside her came a determination to push Darcy away. For a brief moment Liv considered her motivations, but then just as quickly shoved it all aside. Nothing on this planet was forever, and the last thing she needed at the moment was someone interfering in her life.

The following Tuesday morning, Liv dropped Chesney off at the preschool and reminded the teacher that her daughter would be staying for the whole day rather than the typical half day. Adrenalin dripped excitement into her veins as she rushed to a local pastry shop to meet Debbie for breakfast before they headed out for a day of fun.

The light ahead of her turned red, so Liv slowed to a stop, her thoughts once more returning to her weekly outings with Debbie, a relatively new member of their small group of military wives whose husbands were all in the same squadron. While Darcy was slow and steady and full of compassion, Debbie was full of energy and life, with the looks of a super model. She always seemed happy and composed, like nothing ever got her down.

A few minutes later, Liv pulled up outside a quaint bakery not far from Pensacola NAS. Debbie's fire-engine red Corvette was already there.

Inside, Liv gave her eyes a chance to adjust to the darkness, and finally spotted Debbie already at a booth near the back.

Liv made her way through the obstacle course of occupied tables and slid into the faux leather seat across from her fashionable friend. "Sorry I'm late."

"No worries." Debbie sent a Colgate grin that vied for position with the Florida sun. "I hope it's okay, but I went ahead and ordered us some bagels." She patted her non-existent tummy flab. "Have to watch the waistline."

Liv pushed aside her lingering desire for an oversized cinnamon roll. Yes, she needed to watch her weight.

Especially with the new baby coming and the leftover pounds from Chesney's birth. "Sounds good. What's on the agenda for the day?"

Debbie's dark eyes twinkled with excitement. "My goal is to cheer you up. So I planned us a spa day, complete with massages and head-to-toe makeovers. After that, I thought we'd head out for some Christmas and clothes shopping, and lunch at that new bistro. I hear their mixed drinks are wonderful."

Mixed drinks? Liv pasted a pseudo-smile on her face. She hadn't divulged her secret to anyone, so Debbie had no way of knowing that alcohol was on her "don't do it" list. Her thoughts returned to Debbie's other plans for the day. And to her overly expensive tastes. Exactly how much was all this fun and excitement going to cost her?

Later that afternoon, Liv stared at her almost unrecognizable reflection in the dressing room of yet another designer boutique Debbie had dragged her to. Yes, the dress was beautiful and the perfect compliment to the new tawny streaks in her now non-frizzy hair. It would also be the perfect "welcome home" dress for when Jeff returned stateside. But she'd already bought two dresses, a pair of skinny jeans she had absolutely no chance of fitting in with her burgeoning belly, and had even splurged on designer gifts for family members that they probably didn't want or need. And to make matters worse, she had bought none of the winter or maternity clothes they actually needed, and the credit cards she and Jeff had worked so hard to pay off once more inched ever closer toward Never-never Land.

Disgusted with herself, Liv yanked the clingy dress over her head and tossed it to the nearby silken bench. Within a few minutes, she was once more dressed in her normal attire and outside the dressing room where Debbie waited in a cushy chair.

"The dress didn't work?"

Liv shook her head. "Nope." That wasn't a lie. The price alone didn't work.

Her friend frowned. "Hmm. I was almost positive that was the most perfect dress for you. I wish you would have showed it to me before changing clothes."

Too bad. Liv held in a disgusted sigh. While at first this outing with Deb had been fun and relaxing, now the endless shopping wore on her nerves to the point she feared snapping.

Debbie elegantly raised her tall, skinny frame from the over-stuffed and luxurious chair. "Ready to hit the next boutique?"

"Mm, sure." *Lord, please get me out of this.* She followed Debbie out the front door and toward the red convertible. They'd just reached the car when her cell phone jangled its "School Days" tune. Liv frowned and dug around in her bag for the phone. Why would the school be calling? She climbed in the passenger side with an apologetic expression to Deb. "Sorry, this is the school, so I have to take it. Hello?"

"Hi, Liv. This is Melissa from The Ark Christian Preschool. I just got word from the school nurse that Chesney is running a fever. I know you'd made other plans for this afternoon, but can you send someone to pick her up?"

Her eyes widened. Whoa, that was one fast answer to prayer. She swallowed and sent Debbie yet another apology with her eyes. "No problem. It might take me a while to get there, but I'll come pick her up. Thanks for calling."

The typical smile on Debbie's lips had faded, but she said nothing, her eyes hidden behind the over-sized designer sunglasses.

Liv dropped her phone back in her bag and turned toward her friend"Chesney has a fever, so I need to go pick her up."

Debbie just nodded and put the gently purring car into gear. "That's exactly why I decided not to have kids. They cramp your style in so many ways."

Not sure of how to respond, Liv simply stared out the passenger side window all the way back to her parked minivan. Her dingy-but-serviceable van was yet another testimony to her boring life as compared to Deb's carefree and unencumbered lifestyle.

# Six

Friday morning, after she'd dropped Chesney off at school and returned back home, Liv quickly clicked through the news headlines that accompanied her email inbox, scouring each article for some small bit of news that might relate to her husband. More beheadings committed against Christians in the Middle East at the hands of jihadists. More back and forth news of an economy that still bore signs of fragility brought on by the Twin Towers incident of 2001. More school shootings and church burnings. What was happening to their once relatively peaceful world?

She frowned and clicked out of the frightening news and on her inbox, then quickly scanned the contents, without finding what she hoped to see. Another morning with no email from Jeff. While it wasn't entirely unusual for him to miss a couple of days of communicating with her, it did cause concern, especially in light of the world's bad news. What would happen to her and Chesney and their unborn child if he were killed in the line of duty?

Familiar anxiety uncurled snaky tentacles and encased her heart, squeezing it tight. That's exactly what had prompted her to start her own photography business right after Jeff had left. It was too soon to see if the move would be profitable, but at least it offered some measure of hope.

While Chesney had played at the beach this past Sunday, Liv used the time to capture photos of the beach. Devoid of summer vacationers, the area beaches resounded with peaceful sounds of ocean waves, crying gulls, and gentle winds. A sort of wild beauty of the beach they'd visited had captured Liv's awe and wonder as she'd snapped photo after photo of ocean waves, gnarled oak trees, and dead wood bleached white by the relentless sun and salty sea air.

She'd uploaded some photos to various sites on the web, hoping they'd bring in a few bucks and get her work noticed. In addition, she'd built a simple website and started a Facebook page for her new business, LT's Photography. And just yesterday, a friend of a friend had called about her photographing a beach wedding in early December.

Liv stretched out taut neck muscles by twisting her head from side to side. At least maybe it would help pay off the hundreds of dollars of credit card debt she'd racked up. And hopefully before Jeff returned home.

She glanced at the clock. Time to leave for her first pottery class. Yes, it was yet another expense, but her purpose was two-fold. First, she wanted to create Christmas mugs for every member of her family--like those she'd found on Etsy--mugs that announced her good news at the bottom of each cup. Just the thought brought a smile to her face. Secondly, if she mastered pottery-making, maybe she could create items to sell online at some point down the road.

Fifteen minutes later, Liv pulled up outside the storefront where The Potter's Hand pottery shop was located. She hurried inside and wound her way through the aisles of hand-tossed ceramic pottery and into the back room where Mr. Guthrie sat behind one of two pottery wheels.

He lifted his white head as she entered the room and eyed her over the top of his half glasses. Bushy white eyebrows rose to greet her, and a kind smile tugged his mouth up at the corners. "Well, hello, Liv. Ready for your first class?"

Liv nodded, more than a little nervous. "Definitely. I hope I'm at least somewhat good at this." A shaky laugh followed.

He stood, rinsed off slimy clay fingers, dried his hands on a towel, then walked toward her with a hand outstretched. "You'll do fine."

She clasped his hand in her own. "Thanks for making room for me in your schedule, Mr. Guthrie."

"Call me Marty. Happy to do so. Now tell me more about these cups you're wanting to learn how to make."

Liv reached for her Smartphone and quickly pulled up the picture she'd found online. "I'm expecting our second child and wanted to find a unique way to break the news to my family when we're together for Christmas."

His smile broadened. "Congratulations. Nothing like a baby to bring joy and peace. I call 'em instant blood pressure medication." He released a gentle cackle and eyed the picture on her phone through the bottom of his glasses which sat halfway down his button nose. "Cute idea. I think that's definitely do-able by the middle of December." He motioned to the stool behind the second potter's table. "Have a seat and let's get started."

With much attention to detail, he talked Liv through the process of wedging and throwing the clay. Then he demonstrated how to shape the cup as the wheel turned, expertly drawing the clay up vertically until a handle-less cup emerged.

Eager to give it a try, Liv followed the same steps as Marty, but instead of shaping the cup, the clay collapsed to one side, creating more of a school child's artwork than the pretty Christmas mugs she'd envisioned. She released disgust through her nose. "Why doesn't mine look like yours?"

Marty laughed, his blue eyes a-twinkle. "Because I've had years of practice. Don't give up. You'll get the hang of it."

For the rest of their time together, Liv tried again and again to fashion a cup. Her last attempt of the day came the closest to resembling a cup without a handle, but nothing she'd care to give as a gift. Before she left, Marty once more demonstrated the process with the marred clay. A beautiful cup emerged once more.

Liv thanked him for his time, promised to return at the scheduled time the following week, and headed toward home, her mind on the pottery lesson. The process wasn't as easy as Marty Guthrie made it look. How he could take the same piece of clay that had produced nothing but flawed pottery in her hand and fashion it into a beautiful shape still awed her. Maybe she could indeed learn to make the cups in time for Christmas. And maybe--just maybe-- God could take the broken pieces of her current life and mold it all into something beautiful. How, she didn't know, but if anyone was able, God was.

"Get a move on it, Missy." Liv playfully swatted her daughter's behind with the bath towel later that night. "We're already late for bedtime, so if you want a story you'd better hurry it up."

Chesney quickly donned her pajamas, eyes shining. "Will you tell me a story from the big story? I can't wait to see what happens next."

Liv smiled, happy this approach seemed to be working. "That depends. Do you remember what happened last time?"

Damp red curls bouncing, her daughter nodded. "Yeah. Adam and Eve listened to the snake's lies, and disobeyed God's rule about the tree. They had to leave the perfect place God made for them."

A few minutes later, Chesney and Liv once more reclined against the headboard of Chesney's bed. Liv opened her Bible. "Adam and Eve had two sons named Cain and Abel. Cain got jealous and angry at Abel, so he killed him. The world got so evil that God was sorry he had made man. He found a man named Noah who pleased him, so God told to Noah to build..." She intentionally broke off her sentence.

"The ark!" Chesney's face glowed with her accomplishment.

"Very good." Liv gave her daughter a high five. "After the flood, God put a promise of peace in the sky. Do you remember what that was?"

"Yep. A bee-U-ti-ful rainbow." Her daughter comically over-pronounced the word, her arms spread open wide.

Liv's thoughts immediately returned to her pottery making session. The story of Noah and the rainbow was a perfect example of how God could take a mess and bring about good. But what had to be destroyed for it to happen in her life?

"Mommy, you said the rainbow was a promise of peace. What is peace?" Chesney's eyes held curiosity.

Good question. Liv's mind shuffled through potential answers. "Well, people would probably say that peace is no war or bad feelings." But as usual, people's definitions weren't always what God had in mind. "And in the story of Noah's Ark it was a promise not to destroy the world with another flood."

"Is that all peace is?"

Obviously her young daughter didn't think so. Liv's thoughts returned to a discussion she'd had earlier that day with her mother on the topic of peace. How had she worded it?. "That may be part of it, but I think God would say that peace is the total wholeness and complete well-being of people in a right relationship with Him." Even as the words rolled from her lips from some place deep inside her, Liv knew her relationship with God wasn't what it was supposed to be. In her hurt and resentment, she'd pushed Him away. And somehow she needed to turn things right-side up again. But how? She gulped down the hard knot in her throat and looked over at her daughter.

Chesney's eyes glazed over with the obvious need for sleep, so Liv closed her Bible, tucked her daughter under the covers, and quietly left the room, closing the door behind her. The discontinued train of thought over her relationship with God returned with sharp intensity. She released a weary sigh, the fatigue from her pregnancy and single parenting efforts muddling her brain. *God, I don't know how to fix things, and I'm too tired to even try. Please show me what I can do, and give me the strength to do it.*

Liv made her way to the living room. A few minutes later she curled her legs to one side on the sofa and began clicking through television channels. Another typical long dragging night of life without her husband.

# Seven

L iv brought a hand to her chest as though to stop the frantic pounding. "Please tell me this is some kind of sick joke and not the truth." She spoke the words into her phone with a nauseating feel in the pit of her stomach.

"I wish I could tell you that, Liv, but Doug Skyped me last night. Debbie's husband was killed in Afghanistan." Darcy's voice held sorrow, and even through the phone, Liv could tell she was crying. "I knew you and Debbie had become good friends, so I called you first. She's going to need you to help her through this."

Liv's thoughts went to her self-confident friend. If anyone could handle this, Debbie could. Right?

"There's more."

Her heart pounded even more furiously, until Liv thought it might rip itself from her chest. Was Jeff safe? "What?"

"Joan's husband is apparently coming home, but from what Doug said, he is not the same person."

Liv's knees buckled beneath her and hit hard against the cold tile floors. Tears began to flow down her cheeks. How could any of them survive any more destruction.

"You still there, Liv?"

Somehow she found enough of her voice to whisper a husky "Yeah."

"I'm going to reach out to Joan. Will you do the same for Debbie?"

How she didn't know, but she had to try. Darcy was right. For whatever reason, she and Debbie had clicked. Now Debbie needed her. "Yes."

"I'll talk to you later."

All Liv could do was nod. She dropped the phone to the floor and buried her face against her palms, sobs racking her body. After several minutes, she pulled herself from the floor with phone in hand and called her mom. She'd know the best way to approach the situation.

"Hi Liv. What's up?"

The story spilled from her lips. "What should I do to help Debbie, Mom? I feel like I'm barely holding on in all this, and I'm not sure I have anything to say or do that will help." Her words still trembled with barely-contained emotion.

A heavy sigh sounded through the phone. "The best thing you can do is to give her a safe place to mourn. It won't be easy, but God will help you."

Liv swallowed. "That's another thing. I've been so upset at God that I've shut Him out. I don't feel like my relationship with Him is what it should be. So how can I help someone else?"

"Life is full of yuck, Liv. I know I don't have to tell you that, because you're living with a lot of it at the moment."

She paused. "But you can't get stuck in the yuck. That's no way to live."

A surprising smile curved her lips ever so slightly. Chesney would love that terminology. "But what can I do to get out of it?" The yuck was like quicksand. Once it grabbed hold, it sucked you down further and further until escape seemed impossible.

"The best thing to do is live in the possibilities and hope God gives, while at the same time being grateful and realistic."

Live in hope. Be grateful, but also realistic. Great advice, but incorporating it wouldn't be easy.

"I know that's not easy, but it's the truth. Another thing that helps is to stop focusing on the storm and instead focus on the Stiller of Storms. Seek after God, not answers. He will help you."

Yes, that was great advice. Not easy, but definitely true. For the first time since Darcy's disturbing phone call, she felt a little more at peace. "Thanks, Mom. I knew you could help."

A tender laugh sounded. "That's what moms are for." Again her mother paused. "I'm not quite sure how to say this, Liv, but it needs to be said."

"It's okay. Say it."

"It's easy in your situation to focus on yourself. And while a little bit of self-care is needed, don't go too far with it. One of the best ways to stay out of your own yuck is to help others through theirs."

Liv gave her mother's words quick consideration. "More good advice, Mom. I just hope I can carry through with it." After all, how could you see through the dark fog of your own pain to help others? Wasn't that just another case of the blind leading the blind?

All day Liv struggled between the need to call Debbie and the reluctance to do so. On one hand, she truly wanted to help, but wouldn't her own pain and fear only make matters worse? Several times she picked up her phone, but each time failed to follow through. Later that night, she sat down with Chesney to continue the story. "Abraham, Isaac, Jacob, and Judah--as good as they could sometimes be-- were also broken people, just like all the ones who had come before them." Liv could see questions in her young daughter's eyes.

"Did God glue them back together like when I broke that little statue on your dresser?"

Liv laughed. "Well, He helped them through their brokenness, but He also made promises to them--just like he did to Adam and Eve--that the Fixer would come through their family some day. They waited and waited for the Fixer to come during their lifetimes, but everyone of them died without the promise coming true."

A sudden flash of anger lit Chesney's eyes. "You always tell me not to make promises I can't keep."

"That's true. But God didn't break the promise. He just delayed in sending the promise."

"But why?"

Liv shrugged. "I guess because He wanted people to learn to trust Him to do what He said He'd do. Besides that, it might not have been time. God sees everything, and He loves us very much. So I'm sure He had good reasons." She skewed her lips to one side and tried to think of an analogy. "It's like the promise Daddy gave you before He left. He told you that he'd be back. He hasn't broken his promise. It's just not time yet."

Now Chesney's eyes turned sorrowful. "Yeah, but it already feels like a year."

Liv ducked her head before her daughter could see the quick tears that had gathered in her own eyes. "Yes, it does."

"And Daddy might not come back."

Her head snapped up. "What do you mean?"

"A.J. told me that sometimes soldiers die in war."

Her throat constricted. What could she say to alleviate a fear in her daughter that also resided in the depths of her own soul?

"Mommy, why does God let the devil keep lying to people and making them mess up?"

Liv shifted her weight. How could she say this in a way Chesney could understand? "Well, first of all, we're the ones who decide to listen to the lies and act on them. Yes, the devil lies to us, but we have the choice to do the right thing. Secondly, God sometimes lets the devil tell us lies as a sort of test."

"Where we either pass or fail?" A horrific expression took up residence on her daughter's face. "Oh no! I'll never be good enough."

Liv hugged her tight to bring comfort. "None of us are good enough or will ever be good enough. But it's not a pass or fail test. It's more like a test to see if we'll do the right thing. A test to take the bad stuff out of us and make us more like Jesus." She paused to collect her thoughts. "With every good choice we make--to not listen to the lies and end up with another broken piece--God makes us more like Jesus and uses us to help others."

"With their broken pieces?"

"Exactly." As Liv tucked her daughter in and kissed her goodnight, one thought alone churned in her mind. How like God to use His Word and her daughter's innocent words to prod her in the direction she'd needed to go all day long.

With her heart in her throat, but resolve in her spirit, she moved to the living room, picked up her phone, and called Debbie.

# Eight

The next day Liv dropped Chesney off at school, then drove to Debbie's as she had promised her the night before. All the way, she thought and prayed through possible words to say, but by the time she reached her friend's house, she still felt at a loss of what to say or do.

With her knees quivering, Liv made her way to the front door and rang the doorbell.

Footsteps and then the deadbolt clicking sounded from within. The door swung open to reveal a very different Debbie.

Liv did all she knew to do, and that was to engulf Debbie in her arms as her friend broke into sobs, clinging to Liv as if her life depended on it. Once her tears were spent, she backed away, head lowered, dabbing her face with her palms.

"I know you're not used to seeing me like this." Debbie looked at her through puffy red eyes, her face still moist with tears.

Liv smiled. "You're right. But you know what? Now you seem real."

A surprising chuckle sounded from Debbie. She brought both hands into the air and swung them down both sides of her body. "This is as real as I get." Then she swiveled and motioned for Liv to follow her. "C'mon, I have coffee and doughnuts in the kitchen."

Just minutes later, the two reclined on Debbie's lush white sectional sofa over doughnuts and coffee.

Liv's brain scrambled to find words. "I'm so sorry this happened." That was the best she could do?

Debbie smiled through tears. "Thank you." She paused a moment. "I just don't know what to do or where to go from here."

Liv took a bite of the warm Krispy Kreme doughnut and let it dissolve in her mouth. Better to just let Debbie talk rather than pound her with a bunch of questions.

"I don't even have a job. That's one thing I always resented about being a military wife." She took a sip of her coffee, then sat the cup on the glass-topped coffee table. "Mike always got to follow his career dreams, while I always got to follow Mike."

Liv's chest tightened in pain. Hadn't she always felt the same way at times? "I totally understand, Debbie. When Jeff left this last time, I started a photography business. I'm afraid of losing him and not having anything else to fall back on." There. She'd given words to her fear. But rather than feel better, she felt as though she was just spreading the fear around and making it multiply.

Tears leaked from pooled eyes and dripped down Debbie's cheeks. "At least you have a child. A piece of your husband that I'll never have from mine."

"I thought you didn't want kids."

"I didn't. But I sure do now." Debbie yanked a Kleenex from a box between them on the couch and dried her eyes, all the while shaking her head in desperation. "What am I supposed to do?"

Liv's shoulders rose and fell as she released a sigh. Just as she'd expected. She had nothing. Nothing to help someone whose world had exploded into pieces. No words. No emotional Band-Aid. Words fell from her lips without permission or thought. "It's been good to have my family and my daughter, but without God, I'd fall apart." Where had that come from?

Before her very eyes, Debbie's once-friendly face morphed into a hard shell of a mask. "Boy, am I easily deceived. I didn't take you for one of them." She rose to her feet.

Liv frowned. One of them?

"I think it's time for you to go." Debbie refused eye contact.

She stood. "I'm sorry if I said something wrong. I was just trying to help."

A scornful laugh came from her friend. "Doubtful. You just wanted to use my pain to make me fall for a pack of lies." Debbie strode to the front door.

A pack of lies? Is that how Debbie saw the Bible? Liv followed and arrived just as the door opened as a command for to her to leave. She stopped and faced Debbie, her heart heavy. "I'm sorry if that's what you think. I wanted to help because you're my friend."

"Not any more." The words dripped like frozen icicles.

Liv stepped out the door and turned once more. "Please don't do this, Debbie. Let me help."

Debbie's swollen eyes narrowed to narrow slits. "I don't need that kind of help. By the way, I got word through the grapevine that there are two men from our squadron missing in action. Do you know where your husband is?"

With those fear-filled words still hanging in the air between them, the door slammed in Liv's face, her mind and heart immediately focused on her worst fears.

With an aching chest and frantic thoughts, Liv made her way back home as quickly as possible. Was it true? Or was Debbie in such a place of pain that she wanted others to hurt, too?

Once at home, she threw her purse on the couch and headed straight for the laptop. Email was the top priority in her own frantic version of triage. Had Jeff written? She quickly pulled up the internet and scrolled through her messages. Still nothing from her husband, which did nothing but exacerbate her panic. Next she googled "missing in action in Afghanistan." There were plenty of stories--even some that were recent--but no details that provided the information she was desperate for.

Liv raised both palms to her cheeks, her breath coming in uneven and shallow spurts. *God, I don't know what to do. Please help me..*

She stood and paced across the floor to the front door and back again, her thoughts racing. The Navy would contact her if he were missing. That tidbit of information floated to the front of her brain, but it did nothing to alleviate the panic that made her pulse bounce around like a buoy on choppy waves.

Liv rubbed a hand across her lips. An all-too familiar part of deployment training for wives was an order not to watch television or the internet for news. She'd broken that cardinal rule more than once. But now she had to know, and would do anything to find out. She picked up her phone and called Darcy.

"Hey, Liv."

"Hey. Listen I was just over at Debbie's and she said two men were missing in action. Is that true?"

Her friend's shocked gasp sounded through the phone, but other than that the silence was deafening. Finally Darcy broke the silence. "Yes, but I don't know who."

"What do you mean you don't know? How can you know two are missing, but not know who they are?"

"When Doug and I were on Skype, he mentioned that two were missing, but we got cut off before he could tell me who. I haven't heard from him since."

For the second time in two days, Liv's knees buckled beneath her. And a second later, she lost her Krispy Kreme doughnut and cup of coffee.

*Nine*

How was school today?" Liv delivered the question as chipper as possible as her daughter climbed into the back seat and buckled the belt on her car seat. For Chesney's sake she had to maintain a facade of normalcy, even when it seemed like everything was falling to pieces with the news of two missing in action and absolutely no communication from Jeff.

Her daughter's hang-dog expression let Liv know that it hadn't been a good day.

Liv moved around the car, climbed in the driver's seat, buckled her seatbelt, and put the car in gear, easing out of the long line of cars at the preschool. "Wanna talk about it?" She peered in the rearview mirror at Chesney.

"No matter how hard I try to do the right thing, I always mess up." Chesney's overly dramatic hands gestured wildly as she spoke.

"Me too."

Chesney's already big eyes widened further and her lowered chin stretched out her face with lips drawn up tight.

Liv suppressed a smile. "Does that surprise you?"

Her daughter nodded, again with an overdramatic flair. "I thought grown-ups didn't mess up."

"Well, that doesn't line up with the biggest story now, does it? Adam, Eve, Cain...even Abraham. They were all grownups, and they continued to mess up." Mess-ups and broken pieces were deeply embedded in the genetic code of humanity.

"So it's okay to mess up?"

"Yes and no. We should never mess up on purpose just because we can. But when we do mess up, we need to be honest with God and ourselves that we've blown it." Advice Liv had heeded a few minutes before leaving to pick up Chesney, as she poured out her heart and own broken pieces to God, pleading for His help.

"What about the Fixer?"

"What about Him?"

"Does He show up in the next part of the story?"

Liv smiled at her daughter through the rearview mirror, happy her daughter was so into this telling of the gospel story, but wishing against all hope that Jeff would return to help her tell it. "Guess we'll find out later tonight. For right now, how does a trip to the beach sound?"

"Hurray! Let's go to the beach!"

That evening, feeling more relaxed and less panicked after their visit to the beach and dinner out, Liv and Chesney once more reclined on Chesney's bed, Liv's Bible open on her lap. "Tonight the story is about Moses and the people of Israel."

"I know that story," crowed Chesney triumphantly. "Moses' mommy put him in a basket and then in a river so the king's daughter would see him."

"Good for you, Chesney, but this part of the story is when Moses is a grownup."

"Oh." The air in her daughter's sails sagged momentarily, but then a curious light shone in Chesney's eyes. "Was Moses broken too?"

"Definitely. Just like all people are. He even killed a man. In fact, he was living in the desert, trying to hide away from his wrongdoing, when God told him to go back to Egypt where the children of Jacob had become slaves. It would be his job to set the people free from slavery."

"What is slavery?"

"It's when the people in power make others do whatever they say. The Hebrew people had to make bricks and build cities for the wicked king. They cried out to God, and God sent Moses to deliver them."

"Did it work?"

"Yes, in a great and mighty way. God gave Moses the ability to do many signs and wonders. At first the wicked king refused to let the people go, but finally God convinced him." Liv paused to corral her thoughts. This next part was difficult to understand, even as an adult. Would a four-year-old accept it? "The night before the people left, God did something very special. He had all the people kill a lamb to eat. He told them to put some of the blood over their door. Those who listened were saved, but those who didn't experienced death in their houses."

Chesney's normally smooth forehead had wrinkled, and her eyes held sorrow. "Why did they have to kill the lambs?"

"Well, it was what God told them to do, and it provided food for them."

"Couldn't they just go to the grocery store for food to eat?"

A smile burgeoned on Liv's face. Good point. "I know it's hard for you to understand, but back then people grew their own food. But the most important reason for killing the lambs was that it was a picture of what would happen when the Fixer would come." Liv observed her daughter's face. Chesney seemed to not only hang on every word, but also accept it. "The last God-sign was enough for the mean king to let the Hebrew people go."

"I bet they were happy."

"Yes, they were. But it didn't take too long before they started following their own way instead of God's way."

Chesney shook her head back and forth to show that their behavior made no sense to her.

"In fact, God gave ten special rules to show the people how to live in relationship to God and their fellow man, but like you and me, no matter how hard they tried--sometimes because they didn't try at all and sometimes because they made their own rules--they couldn't keep God's law perfectly."

A big yawn crept from Chesney's mouth, in spite of her attempts to stifle it.

Liv closed her Bible. "It's time for you to go to sleep, little one. We'll do some more of the big story later on." As she tucked the covers around her nearly-asleep daughter, her thoughts flashed once more to her daughter's birth. What a miracle that Chesney survived, a reminder for the present that God had a way of working things out when there seemed to be no hope. Now a second miracle child lived within her.

Fear once more tremored through her veins in the enemy's attempt to take over her thoughts and move her focus. Fears about Jeff's safety and his ability to make it home in one piece. Fears about how she would ever be able to bear and raise another child and Chesney, especially if she had to do it on her own. Fears that splintered inside her brain, sending prickly shards that embedded in her flesh. What was it Mom had said? Something about living in the possibilities and hope rather than the yuck. She closed her eyes, suddenly world weary and the enemy close, but God even closer.

Yes, the enemy wanted her to live in the yuck, to give way to her fears, to fall into a depression and hopelessness. But God was bigger, a fact she had to hold on to with every ounce of faith and strength she could muster. Somehow-- even in the midst of her own broken pieces--she had to learn to trust Him more and keep her mind focused on Him.

# Ten

Friday morning, Liv accepted Darcy's offer for help and let her friend drop Chesney off at school so she could make her early morning pottery lesson on time. After the normal greetings, Liv set to work, wedging the clay like she'd learned the previous week. Next she moved to the pottery wheel with the wedged clay. She once more watched Marty Guthrie as he easily demonstrated how to form a cup.

She paid particular attention to his fingers and noticed for the first time how his hands were both gentle and strong. Not too much pressure, but just enough, with each hand exerting an equal amount of strength. Though it took her several tries, by the end of the lesson she had formed an acceptable cup.

"Want to keep this one?" The spry old man peered above the top of his reading glasses.

Liv shook her head and glanced at the clock. She'd have to get a move on it to make her doctor's appointment. "I don't think so. I think I'm finally getting the hang of it, so I'll wait until next week and see how it goes then."

"Sounds good to me."

She thanked him and hurried outside to her minivan. A few minutes later she arrived at the medical clinic with five minutes to spare, but her heart raced from the expended energy and effort.

To her pleasant surprise, she was ushered to the exam room just a few minutes later.

Liv tried not to flinch as Dr. Amy's cool stethoscope landed on her lower abdomen. She watched for any sort of reaction on the doctor's face. Had her fears and worries and stress caused even more problems, especially as it related to the baby?

A slight frown appeared between Dr. Amy's eyes. She listened some more, then sighed, and removed the stethoscope to let it hang around her neck. "How have you been feeling, Liv?"

Liv grimaced. Best not to hold anything back, though she was pretty sure the doctor wouldn't like it. "Not well, actually. My husband deployed right after I found out about the pregnancy. I've been upset, depressed, and struggling to keep a normal life going for our daughter. Then a friend of mine--who is also a military wife--lost her husband." She intentionally left out the part about the soldiers missing in action, doing all she could to follow her mother's advice to live in hope.

The doctor's eyes had taken on compassion, but her lips had drawn into a thin taut line. "And what are you doing to take care of yourself?"

Good question. Liv moved her gaze to the typical suspended ceiling tiles of office buildings. "Does retail therapy count?"

The doctor laughed. "Only if you can afford it."

Another grimace landed on Liv's face. So far she was coming up short. Far short. "I took up pottery and started a photography business."

"Now we're getting somewhere, as long as you don't overdo it with your new business. What about your extended family?"

"They're in Colorado. I thought about taking Chesney to see them over the Christmas holidays." She cast an expectant gaze on the doctor, pleading silently that the idea would be an agreeable one.

"Flying or driving?"

Liv longed to keep the answer to herself, certain the doctor wouldn't approve. "Driving."

Dr. Amy said nothing, but shook her head from side to side.

"I really need some time with them." The words tumbled from Liv's lips in a pleading tone.

"I understand that, and I think it would be good for you emotionally. But based on the baby's erratic heartbeat I don't think it's advisable for you to drive that far." She paused. "I know you're not going to like this, but unless you start doing a better job of dealing with your stress, you'll end up on bed rest for the remainder of your pregnancy."

Liv was immediately struck by the irony of the situation. The thing she most needed right now was time with her family. That would surely help relieve her stress. But because she was so stressed out, she couldn't travel. One vicious circle. No, make that a Ferris wheel. Just how in the world was she supposed to come off the merry-go-round of life in one piece?

As she made her way back home after the doctor's appointment, Liv sent one short prayer--over and over again--to the throne room of grace. *God help me. You're the only One who can.*

"How are you doing?"

Liv sighed. She didn't want her mother to worry, but still it helped to have someone who understood. And she desperately needed that at the moment. "I'm hanging in there. Some days are obviously better than others, but overall it's been a rough week so far."

"How's your friend?"

An acute ache for Debbie lodged in her heart. "Not good. I tried reaching out to her, but when I mentioned God she got very upset and asked me to leave."

"I'm so sorry, Liv. Guess I should've also told you that people don't always respond well to our offer for help, especially when we bring God into the equation." Her mother's heavy sigh sounded through the phone. "A trend that seems to be growing worse by the day. But I'd encourage you to try to keep both the lines of communication and your offer of help open."

Liv nodded. Hadn't she sensed in her quiet time with the Lord that morning that was exactly what He wanted her to do? "I'd already planned on calling her later today."

"But don't get upset with her if she doesn't respond the way you expect. Any sort of relationship takes two willing parties."

Another nugget of wisdom to add to her arsenal. Should she mention that two men from Jeff's unit were MIA? And that she'd had no contact with Jeff in several days?

"Are you and Ches still coming for Christmas?"

Liv paused to consider the question. It all depended on how her pregnancy progressed, news she still hadn't shared with anyone else. "We'll wait and see, Mom. I want to, but I just don't know at this point." Just to speak the words aloud weighed heavy on her heart. And she wasn't ready to divulge the pregnancy to her mother yet, in the off chance that she was able to bring her stress under control and make the drive to Colorado for Christmas.

"Well if you decide you can't swing it, be sure you give me plenty of notice to get Chesney's gift to her."

"I will. What did you get her?"

"I found the cutest pattern for a Santa dress. I picked up some red velvet and white faux fur earlier this week. I'm going to make them for all the granddaughters. But I'd like to put some sort of decoration on the bottom of the skirt that is special to each one. Any ideas for Chesney?"

Liv thought for a moment, and then shook her head. "None that hit me right off the bat, but I'll think on it some more and let you know what I come up with."

After the conversation ended, Liv hurried to the preschool to pick up Chesney. Glorious and sunny, the Friday begged for an outdoor outing. A fact that she'd prepared for in advance, as evidenced by the stale half loaf of bread in the passenger's seat. Once Chesney was securely buckled in, Liv made her way to a nearby park for a special treat for her daughter.

"Mom, where are we going?"

"I thought you might enjoy feeding the ducks and swans at the park." And it might just work wonders for her own disposition as well. At this point--with Christmas growing ever closer and her stress mounting--she was willing to try just about anything.

A happy sigh sounded from the back seat. "I love the swans. They're my favorites."

"Why are they your favorites?"

"Because it's like the story Miss Cindy read to us at school about an ugly duckling. He was upset because he didn't look like the other ducklings. He thought something was wrong with him while everyone else was perfect. It turned out that he wasn't a duck at all, but a beautiful swan, and when he grew up, he was prettier than all the ducks."

Forever on the lookout for teachable moments, Liv uttered the question that had flown into her heart. "And what lesson does that teach us?"

"That we can't make up our mind about someone by seeing them from the outside. Miss Cindy said that God doesn't look at our outsides, but our hearts."

The perfectly-summarized moral to the story that sounded from the backseat had an unexpected impact, and Liv momentarily battled tears. Her baby girl was growing up way too quickly. But in spite of that fact, her heart had been lightened by the child-like reminder to not get caught up in the externals of life. Appearances--even the potential for danger for Jeff--could indeed be deceiving.

A few minutes later they arrived at the park and stepped to the water's edge. Liv handed slices of bread to her daughter and looked on as she happily fed them to the ducks and swans. Her mother's question about what to put on Chesney's Santa dress flew to Liv's thoughts. Now she knew exactly how to answer. She made a mental note to call her mother later that night with the suggestion of swans.

Several hours later, after bath time, Liv once more positioned her back against the headboard of Chesney's bed while her daughter donned her pajamas. Without warning, the memory of her and Jeff sharing the story of Adam and Eve with Chesney trounced into her heart, bringing with it an inexpressible sadness. What she wouldn't give to have Jeff there to snuggle with and to share this special time.

Liv closed her eyes as the familiar picture of Jeff walking in the front door after work came to mind. She could see him and smell him and hear his special greeting of endearment. "Hi, Liv-love." Could feel the soft touch of his lips against her hair. Her eyes stung with tears while a sad smile broke out on her face at just the remembrance of Jeff's voice.

"Mommy, are you okay?" Chesney straddled Liv's knees and placed a palm on both sides of her face.

"Yeah, baby, I'm okay. Just tired."

Mock consternation flooded her daughter's overly-dramatic face. "Did you take a nap today?"

Liv laughed. Always the little mother. "No, but I'll try to remember to do that next time."

Chesney crawled over to her pillow and snuggled under the covers. "Mommy?"

"Yes?"

"How come Daddy hasn't called?"

Her heart landed in her throat, and she did all she could to keep her tone on an even keel. "I'm sure he's just really busy, Ches. You know that's how it is sometimes."

"I know. I was just wondering." Chesney's face took on a faraway look, but then just as quickly returned to normal. "What's the next part of the big story? Does the Fixer finally come?"

Liv shook her head. "Not yet. Believe it or not, the people kept messing up, their lives broken in pieces, sort of like Humpty Dumpty, while they waited for the Fixer to get there."

Chesney frowned. "Why is it so hard to wait for something good?"

The question set off another wave of longing inside Liv. *Lord, please bring Jeff home safely. We're so tired of waiting and not knowing if he's okay.* A prayer she'd prayed at least a thousand times.

The same plaintive longing resonated in Chesney's voice. "You know, like waiting for Christmas and for Daddy to come home."

Liv fought back tears, and beside her, she heard Chesney sniffling. She pulled her daughter into her lap and hugged her tight. "It is hard to wait, but God is with us." The words came out croaky, but at least they came out.

Chesney wiped her eyes and peered up at Liv. "Can you please start the story so I won't be sad any more?

Liv nodded and quickly opened her Bible. Even Chesney knew that focus on God made all the difference. "Sure. Do you remember what we talked about last time?"

Her daughter pulled her lips between her teeth, slanted her eyes to the upper left, and placed an index finger on her chin. "Mmmm, Moses and the ten rules?"

"Good, Chesney. You got it. Ready to learn what happens next?"

Chesney nodded.

"The people wanted to be like the nations around them. Have you ever wanted something that someone else had?"

Chesney thought a moment. "Yeah. Remember when I told you and Daddy about it before he left?"

Liv shook her head. No recollection at all.

Her daughter sent her a reprimanding look. "Think harder, Mommy. A.J. told me that he was getting a kid Jeep for Christmas, you know, the kind that really works 'cause it has a battery, and I told you and Daddy that I wanted one of those, too. Now do you remember?" Chubby hands landed against the bed covers to reveal Chesney's agitation.

A laugh gurgled out of Liv. "Okay, now I remember."

"Can I get one?"

"I guess we'll have to wait and see, won't we? Let's get back to the story. Just like you, the Hebrew people wanted what the nations around them had. But because of that, they wandered further and further away from God and His law. Then they would get in trouble and cry out to God, and He'd send someone to deliver them. It happened over and over again."

Chesney shook her head from side to side, and released a dramatic sigh. "Still broken."

"Yes." So typical for them and her and all people everywhere. "After that they wanted a king like the nations around them."

"Was that a good thing?"

She shook her head from side to side. "No, because God wanted to be their king. But He gave them what they wanted."

"Can I ask another question?"

"Of course, sweetheart."

"How could the Fixer God promised come from such messed-up people? Wouldn't He be messed up too?"

"You would think so, wouldn't you?"

Chesney nodded, but didn't answer.

"Guess that's another case of we'll have to wait and see." She tousled Chesney's still damp hair. "Let's say our prayers and turn off the lights."

"Okay."

"You want to pray, or do you want me to?"

"I'll do it." Chesney jumped down and knelt beside the bed. Liv joined her. "Dear God, we're so sorry for messing up all the time. Thank you for sending the Fixer. Please help us get to that part of the big story soon and bring Daddy home safely 'cause I'm tired of waiting. We love you. In Jesus' name, Amen."

Liv once more bit back tears as she tucked her daughter in and kissed her forehead. That made two people who were tired of waiting.

"Goodnight, Mommy. I love you."

"And I love you, Chesney. Sleep tight, and don't let the bed bugs bite."

"That's a really mean thing to say to a little kid, you know."

There was no containing her laughter. Liv giggled and smiled down at her daughter. "Guess I messed up again."

Chesney sighed dramatically. "We're all just messed-up people."

Liv laughed and stepped from the room. Just as she pulled the door closed, a feeling like none other came over her--a feeling that Jeff was safe and well and would come home to them soon. While part of her was afraid to trust the feeling, another part of her tingled with an unexpected thrill of hope. *God, let it be in time for Christmas. Please.* She'd even give up her white Christmas dreams to have him back home with her and Chesney.

unday afternoon after church, Liv made the drive to
Debbie's house to check on her. Though she'd tried to
call her friend all week, every phone call went to Debbie's
voice mail, which either meant that her friend was
intentionally not answering or that something was very,
very wrong.

As she pulled up outside Debbie's house, she noticed
her friend's red Corvette in the driveway. So her instincts
had been right. Debbie was ignoring her. Liv released a
cleansing breath and tried to still her nerves. *God, Debbie
doesn't want to see me. Show me how I can help her. Give
me the words to say to get through to her.*

Liv's thoughts returned to her morning at church.
Though she didn't care to admit it, her first motivation for
going to church had been a sort of bargaining chip with
God. After all, wasn't it logical to assume that if she tried to
do things His way, He would return the favor? But both the
Life Group session and the worship service had brought
conviction to her heart, and she'd quickly brought it to God.
It had been very uncomfortable to once more confess her
failure and to try to connect with friends after so many
weeks away, but by the time church was over, Liv felt

better and more at peace than she had in a long time. Now if she could just lead Debbie to that peace. To the Prince of Peace.

Steely resolve moved her down the sidewalk, up the steps, and to the front door. She punched the door bell, and once more tried to settle her nerves with a deep breath.

The door swung open. Debbie's expression held no welcome. In fact, there was nothing about Debbie's appearance that even resembled the old Debbie. No smile, no polished image. Just an empty shell.

Knife-like pain seared through Liv's chest, but she somehow managed a shaky smile. "Hi, Debbie. Can I come in?"

"Depends on what you're here for." The words were short and curt.

Liv swallowed. She hadn't prepared enough for the open hostility her friend unleashed in an acidic tone. "I just wanted to see how you're doing and see if there's anything I can do for you."

"As you can see, I'm doing fine. And no, I don't need anything." Without another word, she slammed the door shut in Liv's face for the second time.

Later that day, after a quick lunch with Darcy and her kids, Liv and Chesney returned home where they both succumbed to a nap. Two hours later Chesney awoke and wandered into the living room to snuggle into Liv's lap. "Mommy, can I play in the back yard?"

"Sure, sweetie. Just be sure to stay there." Liv brushed damp hair away from her daughter's forehead. "Want something to drink first?"

Chesney shook her head, and quickly exited the sliding glass doors that led to the back.

Liv forced herself to a standing position and switched off the television. Now that Chesney was awake, she could clean the oven without fear of waking her daughter.

A half hour later, she finished the job and shut the oven door, suddenly aware that Chesney hadn't once re-entered the house for a drink or to get a toy or to go to the bathroom. The thought hurried Liv's feet to the back door.

"Chesney!" Liv yelled her daughter's name into the backyard and scanned the shrubbery near the fence to see if her little girl appeared from her impromptu game of "Scare Your Mother To Death." But Chesney didn't appear. She stepped out the door and into the yard, still calling her daughter's name. Nothing.

Panic dried her mouth and quickened her pulse. Liv rushed back through the house and out into the front yard. She quickly looked around the neighborhood, but no sign of her daughter. "Chesney!" Her voice took on an edge of the hysteria she felt.

At just that moment, a small head covered with wavy red curls popped up from behind a car in the driveway next door, followed by a blond head that belonged to Chesney's friend, A.J. "I'm over here at A.J.'s house, Mommy."

In an attempt to slow her racing heart, Liv drew in a shaky breath. She hurried to where her daughter stood, battling to keep her emotions in check. "Chesney, tell A.J. 'good-bye,' and get inside our house right this minute." She couldn't help the hard edge to her voice.

A few minutes later, back inside the house, Chesney stood, peering up at her mother with huge crocodile tears pooling in her eyes. "I'm sorry, Mommy. I didn't hear you tell me to stay in the back yard."

Liv mentally counted to ten to control her anger, then bent down low, a hand on her daughter's shoulders. "That's because you didn't listen, Chesney. When I told you to stay in the back yard, you were already thinking about what you wanted to do instead of listening to what I said. Mommy was very scared that something bad might have happened to you."

Chesney cocked her head to one side, suddenly curious. "Did the same thing happen to any of the broken people in the story?"

A tender smile splayed itself on Liv's face. "Yes." Her head slanted to one side as she looked at her young daughter. "Tell you what. Why don't you and I make a big batch of chocolate chip cookies while I tell you the next part of the story."

Chesney's face brightened. "That's a great idea."

Liv tweaked her nose. "But...you are still going to be punished for not listening or minding me."

Just as quickly, her daughter's face darkened. "I said I was sorry, and I won't do it again."

"I know, but I want to make sure you learn this lesson. At least for a while, there'll be no playing outside unless I'm out there with you."

Though Chesney's expression momentarily registered a rebellious look, to her credit, she didn't object, but instead headed into the kitchen. "Okay. So what happens next in the story?"

Liv moved to the cabinets to get the ingredients for the cookies. "Well, God sent some very special messengers, called prophets, to the people. Not only to tell them to do the right thing, but also to give them more promises about the Fixer."

"Like what?"

"One of the promises said they could expect the Fixer to be the Prince of Peace."

"There's that word 'peace' again. Now what did you tell me it meant?" Chesney landed her forehead against her palm, and then looked up with excitement as realization dawned. "I know. It means being complete and whole, instead of broken."

A huge smile broke out on Liv's face. Her daughter was putting the special pieces of this story in all the right places. "Very good, Ches. And God gave them even more promises than that."

Chesney's eyes took on wary caution. "They didn't listen, did they?"

Liv shook her head. "No, they didn't. Just like you, they were more concerned about what they wanted to do than listening to God." The kitchen grew quiet as the two measured and mixed, Liv's thoughts on her own broken heart and life. How many times had she not listened to her heavenly Father because of her desire and tendency to go her own way?

"Mommy?"

"What is it, sweetie?"

"Why don't we all do what God wants us to do?"

Liv searched for the right answer, still examining her own heart. "Sometimes people refuse to see that they're broken. And the snake does all he can to keep us from seeing it, because he doesn't want us to know we're broken."

"That mean old snake. Why doesn't he want us to know we're broken?"

The answer came quickly to her heart. "Because if people can't see their brokenness, they don't know that they need a Fixer. And if they don't need a Fixer, they don't need God." The perfect explanation for Debbie's reaction to faith in Christ. Her friend didn't see herself as in need of being fixed. So why would she need God?

# Twelve

L iv and Darcy stood in a tiny group of people as the Navy plane that bore the body of Mike Ugarich touched down. Though it was mid-November and the skies were cloudy, the temps were mild and balmy. Liv glanced over to where Debbie stood, dressed in black and her head lowered. Though surrounded by soldiers, it didn't appear that any family members had come to support her during this time. Liv's heart wrenched within her chest, and she raised her right hand to the area and let it rest there.

The plane taxied to a stop. What if Debbie didn't want them there? Would this only make matters worse between them?

A few minutes later, the honor guard stepped in perfect synchronization as they bore the body of a fallen comrade. They stopped in front of Debbie, who reached out to place her hand on the casket. As her friend leaned her head back to scan the cloud-covered sky, her gaze met Liv's. A grateful smile tugged at sad lips that were perfectly made up, but did nothing to cover the pain her friend certainly felt.

A weight lifted from Liv's shoulders. Maybe this small act of being present for a tough time was enough to bring Debbie around.

After the flag ceremony, they all moved to a small chapel for a brief memorial service, and only afterwards did Darcy and Liv have the opportunity to speak with Debbie.

The grieving woman's red-rimmed eyes held apology. "Thank you both for being here." She clasped Liv's hands in her own gloved hands. "I'm so sorry for the way I treated you, Liv. I know you were only trying to help."

Liv tried to respond, but the lump in her throat wouldn't permit it. Then without warning, a ferocious cramp in her lower abdomen doubled her over, both hands clasping her gut. A groan she couldn't contain escaped her lips. *Lord, please don't take this baby from me.*

"What's wrong?" Darcy had knelt down to make eye contact. Debbie joined her and held Liv's right arm.

This was no time for secrets. "I'm pregnant. I think you need to take me to the emergency room."

"Why didn't you tell me you were pregnant?" Accusation colored Debbie's tone.

"Don't feel like the Lone Ranger, Debbie. She didn't tell me either." Darcy, who was usually so easy-going, stood with arms crossed and a hurt look on her face.

"Please don't be mad at me. I haven't told anyone." Besides, did any of this really matter with the life of her baby at stake?

Debbie's eyes widened. "Not even Jeff?"

"Not even your mother?" Darcy's face also held incredulity.

"I was waiting to surprise everyone with the announcement at Christmas, then Jeff..."

Darcy gasped. "...got deployed." Compassion oozed from her eyes as she hurried over to Liv's bed and gently embraced her. "I'm so sorry, Liv. I knew you weren't quite yourself, but I couldn't figure out why."

Dr. Amy entered the room, her face unusually stern. "The baby is okay."

A collective sigh of relief sounded around the room.

The doctor glanced briefly at both Debbie and Darcy, then turned her gaze to Liv. "You're very fortunate to have been with friends when this happened. There could have been an entirely different outcome."

Liv raised a hand to her neck, lowered her head, and sent a brief prayer of thanksgiving heavenward.

"But I'm putting you on bed rest for the remainder of your pregnancy."

Her mouth gaped open. "But I have a daughter to take care of." This couldn't have come at a worse time.

"We'll help." Debbie spoke the words firmly.

"Yes," agreed Darcy.

For the first time all day, Dr. Amy smiled. "Looks like you're all taken care of."

"But my trip to Colorado--"

"--will not take place."

Immediate tears flooded Liv's eyes. No family. No birth announcement surprises. No snow. And all that on top of her deployed husband, with whom she'd had no recent contact.

"I could drive her." The offer came from Debbie.

Dr. Amy shook her head. "Sorry, it's a no go."

Liv's thoughts flew to her new business. "And I have a photo shoot in a couple of weeks."

"You'll have to cancel." Everything about Dr. Amy screamed "No!" From her stance to the stern set of her lips and the tone of her voice.

Liv laid her head back against the pillow and stared at the ceiling. Add no work and no income to her already long list of don'ts.

Later, back at the house, Debbie and Darcy took care of all her usual chores. Debbie cooked meals while Darcy picked up Chesney and her own kids. While the kids played in the backyard, Liv laid down on the couch while the other two sat nearby.

In her typical planner mode, Darcy sat with a notebook and pen. "Okay, Liv. Let's get all this ironed out for the next couple of months."

Without hesitation, Debbie jumped in first. "I'd be happy to take care of all the meals and spend the nights here."

78

Liv shook her head. "No. That's way too much for you to take on."

Debbie's expression stood staunchly at attention. "It will give me something to do while I try to figure out what's next for me. I insist."

"Well, if you insist." The two shared a smile, the fragile truce between them instantly becoming more pronounced.

"I can come over while the kids are in school to wash clothes and clean." Darcy didn't even look her way, but scribbled furiously in the notebook.

Liv groaned and brought a couch pillow over her face for a moment. A minute later, she uncovered her face and eyed her two friends. "I hate that I'm disrupting your lives like this."

"Puh-lease." Now Darcy's blue eyes shot fire. "You'd do the same for us, and you know it."

She nodded. Yes, she would. That's just how military wives rolled, especially while their husbands were deployed. "I have a couple of spare keys in the drawer beside the refrigerator."

Darcy and her kids left middle of the afternoon. And after dinner, Debbie made her departure as well, but only after cleaning the kitchen and making sure Chesney had her bath.

Once Chesney was finally in bed, Liv allowed herself full vent of her emotions, something she'd felt the need to do since receiving the news that the trip to Colorado wasn't going to happen. Tears fell like they hadn't in a very long time as she once more poured out her heart to God and cried herself to sleep.

## Thirteen

The following morning Liv awoke in a better frame of mind. Out of sheer exhaustion, she'd slept the entire night, something that hadn't happened since before she got the news that Jeff would be deployed. From the kitchen she smelled breakfast cooking, evidence that Debbie was already here. She smiled and pulled herself to a sitting position. Maybe bed rest wouldn't be so bad after all, especially if she could look at it as being on vacation with a private chef, chauffeur, and housekeeper.

Her happy mood dissipated somewhat at the thought. If that were true, it would be much easier to accept than adding more to her friends' busy schedule. Just as quickly, she was reminded of how badly things could have turned out the previous day. She breathed out another prayer of gratitude for the baby's safety, resolved to do a better job for her and her family. Why had she been so focused on her own hurt and resentment than taking care of her family? The smells and sounds from the kitchen raised her head once more. "Hello? Debbie, is that you?"

Debbie appeared in the doorway a second later. "Well, it's about time you woke up, sleepyhead." A kind smile appeared on her face. "Looks like you rested well. Darcy has taken Chesney to school. I'm here to fix you breakfast and lunch. Darcy has lined up some ladies from church to fill in as needed. Ready for some pancakes?"

Liv didn't object, suddenly overwhelmed by the unselfishness and graciousness of so many. The miraculous change in Debbie was also a point of thanksgiving. Previously, her friend's carefree lifestyle had always seemed a little on the self-centered side, though also enviable. "I'm sorry about this, Debbie. I didn't mean to be a burden to anyone."

Debbie just smiled, but turned and left the room. A few minutes later she was back with two plates of pancakes, one of which she handed to Liv. "About you being a burden, you're not. I don't mind at all. To be honest, I'm grateful."

Liv took a bite of the pancakes and let them melt away in her mouth. She sighed in satisfaction. "These are the best pancakes I've ever tasted. Why didn't you tell me you were such a great cook?" She took another bite. And another.

"First let me finish what I was saying. Then I'll tell you how I learned to cook." She hesitated, as though uncomfortable. "And if you don't mind, I'd also like to run a business idea past you to see what you think."

"Sure." Liv continued to eat. Man, she was going to gain weight like crazy if all Debbie's meals were this good.

"I'm grateful for this time. Helping you takes my mind off my own problems and makes me feel good. And trust me, I haven't felt that way in a very, very long time." Debbie's eyes filled with happy tears.

That was enough to make Liv stop eating the scrumptious pancakes. Against doctor's orders, she slid from the bed, stepped to where Debbie stood, and hugged her neck. "Then I will forever be grateful for the doctor ordering bed rest."

Both of them laughed as Liv crawled back into bed. Debbie launched into talk about how she'd learned to cook and her desire to open a small cafe in downtown Pensacola. Her voice grew more excited as she revealed her plan to open her own business.

"I think it sounds like a great idea." Liv kept her gaze glued on her friend. How she wanted Debbie to be encouraged and find hope. "You could also look into catering and a food truck."

Debbie's perfectly manicured brows shot upward, and she nodded. "I hadn't even thought of those two options."

From her position in bed, Liv saw Debbie's wheels start to turn. The two talked and dreamed for almost an hour before Liv eventually gave way to the drowsiness that seemed to dog her steps nowadays.

That afternoon, after lunch, Chesney burst through the bedroom door, her pink backpack flying behind her. "Guess what, Mommy?"

"What, doll?" Liv tugged her daughter into her arms and kissed her cheek.

"We're going to do a Christmas program, and I'm an angel."

Type-casting at its finest. Liv smiled. "That sounds wonderful." She latched onto Chesney's hand and swung it back and forth.

Chesney yanked her hand away, unzipped her bag, and rummaged through it. "I have a note in my bag from Miss Cindy. She said she needs volun...um, volun..."

"Volunteers?"

"Yeah, that!" Her eyes took on a pleading look. "Can you be what Miss Cindy needs?"

Discomfort rose inside Liv. How unfair that this bed rest would derive her and her daughter of this very special and precious opportunity. And how did she explain it to Chesney in a way she could understand? Another sudden thought rained down on Liv. In addition to telling Chesney, she somehow had to let her Mom know this latest turn of events, and that she and Chesney wouldn't be coming for Christmas after all. She'd put it off long enough.

Darcy entered the room. "Not sure the doctor will let your mom out of bed to volunteer, Ches, but maybe she can make decorations or invitations."

Liv smiled her appreciation. Leave it to Darcy to make them both feel better with a great way to follow doctor's orders and help with the preparations.

Later that night, Chesney snuggled up next to Liv on the couch, obviously eager for the next part of the story. Debbie sat nearby crocheting an afghan.

Liv's thoughts carried her away for a moment. Debbie had never shown any sort of craftiness in all the time they'd known one another. "You don't strike me as the crocheting type." The words popped from her mouth unexpectedly.

Thankfully, Debbie laughed at the spur-of-the-moment comment. "I haven't done it in a very long time, but I'm enjoying it. Gives me something to do with my hands and head. You know, to keep me from thinking too much on the wrong things."

A smile pulled Liv's lips apart. Pretty, talented, and smart. There was more to Debbie than just a beautiful exterior. Liv sent up a silent prayer. *Lord, let Debbie hear this most special part of the big story. Let her heart be opened to receive it and You.*

Liv opened her Bible. "Finally it happened, Chesney."

"The Fixer?" Her daughter's eyes held wonder.

"Yes. Just like God's promises had said it would. He sent a Fixer to take care of all the mess-ups of people who had ever lived and all the people who would live. He came to earth as a baby boy and was laid in a manger."

"What's a manger?"

An amused expression appeared on Debbie's face, but she said nothing as she continued to crochet.

Liv thought through possible answers. "Mmmm...well, it's sort of like a horse trough."

"What's that?"

"A horse eats out of it." Debbie muttered the words, but didn't look up from her work.

"The Fixer was born in a stinky old barn?" Chesney's nose wrinkled. "Why would God do that?"

Now Debbie looked up. "Great question."

Liv shifted her gaze from Debbie to Chesney. "It was part of God's plan. There were lots of things that were special and different about Jesus."

Her daughter's eyes grew big and round. "Jesus is the Fixer?"

"Yes, and He brought lots of surprises during His time on earth."

"Like what?"

"Like miracles and wonderful teaching." Liv paused, searching for the right words. "But the most special thing was that He came to die for our mess-ups."

Debbie stopped crocheting, but her eyes were fixed, as though staring at nothing in particular.

"Die?" Chesney's eyes grew bright with tears. "But if Jesus came to fix messed-up people why did He have to die?"

"I know it's hard to understand, sweetie, but remember when I told you that the lamb the people killed to escape slavery was a picture?"

Chesney nodded.

"Jesus would fix people and fix their broken relationship with God by being the Lamb. By dying, He fixed things for the people once and for all."

A solitary tear fell from one eye. Chesney quickly flicked it away. "But that's not fair."

"No, it isn't. But God knew people could never be good enough on their own. So Jesus--who was really God--chose to die for people and their sins. In this way, He fulfilled the promise to be our Prince of Peace."

"And our broken pieces."

Debbie sniffed briefly and scratched the corner of one eye, but didn't offer an explanation.

Yes, and the broken pieces. Of everyone. A verse she'd memorized years ago immediately flooded Liv's mind. *All we like sheep have gone astray. We've turned, every one, to his own way. But the LORD has laid on Him the iniquity of us all.* Jesus died for all the broken pieces--for all the broken people--in the world.

"So Jesus died forever and ever?"

Chesney's innocent question tugged Liv from her deep thoughts. "No, Chesney. That's one of the best parts of the story. He came back to life. Lots of people saw Him and wrote down what they saw, so we know it's a true story. They talked and walked and ate with Him before He went back to heaven."

"Amazing."

Liv had to smile. Here of late, Chesney used that word to describe just about everything. She glanced over to where Deb worked furiously with the yarn and metal hook. Even with her head lowered her frown was evident. Joy trickled throughout Liv. Debbie had heard every word of the story. She turned back to Chesney. "Yes, it was truly amazing. It was an unusual way for the Fixer to beat the snake and His lies, but it worked. Before Jesus went back to heaven, He promised that His Spirit would live in the people who trusted Him to fix their broken pieces. He also promised them something else."

"What?"

"His peace. He said this." Liv turned to the book of John. *"Peace I leave with you; my peace I give you. I do not give to you as the world gives. Do not let your hearts be troubled and do not be afraid."*

"That makes me feel good on the inside." A gentle smile curved Chesney's mouth. "It makes me not be afraid so much."

"What are you afraid of?"

"Sometimes I get scared that something will happen to Daddy, and I won't get to see him again."

The air in the room thickened with tension. Debbie stopped her furious work and sat perfectly still, her head still lowered.

The lump in Liv's throat made it impossible to speak-- her own fears for Jeff's safety verbalized so perfectly. Instead, she just held her daughter closer.

And prayed for all of them.

# Fourteen

L iv awakened early Sunday morning, the house still quiet and uneventful. She sat up and peered around the room. The sun was just starting to peek through the blinds, throwing slats of light across the bedspread. Being careful to take things easily--something she'd faithfully practiced since her scary visit to the emergency room--Liv made her way to the bathroom and then over to the bedroom window to peer out at the sunrise. Gorgeous streaks of orange and peach and pink painted the sky.

"Thank You, God." The words flowed, unrehearsed, from a grateful heart. He had not only given her this beautiful sunrise, but had spared the life of her unborn child and given her the opportunity to start over and do things right.

Liv moved back to the bed and pulled her Bible into her lap. The wake-up call she'd received had brought disappointing news, but even in just a few short days, it had also reinstated the sweet intimacy in her relationship with God. Now physically unable to distract herself with other things, Liv had turned to Him through His Word and prayer.

No wonder she felt so much better. Instead of focusing on her problems and pieces, she'd focused on God, not for the purpose of answers, but just because of who He was. Proclaiming His love, mercy, grace, goodness, sovereignty, and so much more had brought unfathomable peace. And to think, that peace had always been hers for the taking. It was just a matter of putting on her spiritual armor and keeping her attention focused on God, the only One able to fix her situation and her restless heart.

A sudden thought brought a heavy sigh. Although she'd called and cancelled the photography sessions and at least one week of her pottery lessons, she still hadn't gathered the courage to call her mother, with both the bad news of the broken trip plans and the good news of the baby she carried. Why had she put it off? The answer instantly appeared. She hadn't wanted to verbalize that her dream of a white Christmas with her family just wasn't going to happen. Hadn't wanted to admit that her dream of delivering the news wouldn't be realized, at least as far as her mother was concerned.

Later that morning, after Darcy had picked up Debbie and Chesney for church, Liv called her mother, grateful for the time difference that allowed her this time alone.

"Hi, honey. Is everything okay?"

Even through the phone, Liv recognized the concern in her mother's voice. "I'm fine, Mom, but I have some news."

"I'm so relieved. Earlier this week I was so burdened to pray for you. I guess the Lord knew you needed it. Now what's your news?"

Liv smiled. How like God to lay her needs on the hearts of His prayer warriors. "Do you want the good news or bad news first?"

A short laugh sounded. "I hate those kind of questions. Give me the bad news first, so the good news will make it all better."

Now Liv laughed. That sounded exactly like something Chesney would say. She inhaled deeply, then released the breath and words in one fell swoop. "We're not going to be able to come for Christmas."

"Why not?" Even over the phone, her mother's disappointment was evident in her tone.

"Well, that's the good news part. I'm expecting another baby."

Squeals of excitement and yells to her father filled the phone to the point that Liv had to pull the it away from her ear. Finally her mother calmed down enough to speak. "How long have you known?"

"For a while. I had some problems this week, so the doctor has confined me to bed rest."

"Oh honey, I"m so sorry. I know this trip meant a lot to you. It meant a lot to us, too. But there is no better reason to have to stay home in bed."

A heavy curtain of gloom descended once more on Liv's heart. "I know, but I so wanted to be there. Please don't tell anyone else that I'm pregnant. I'm hoping to make gifts to send to surprise everyone." If she could figure out a new gift other than the mugs. Yet another negative for being confined to bed. No pottery lessons.

"Does Jeff know?"

Liv released a slow breath. "No. I was hoping he'd be home in time for me to surprise him, too." She paused. Should she reveal the greatest fear in her heart? "I...I haven't heard from him in a few weeks, so I'm worried."

"Oh, sweetheart, why didn't you tell me so I could at least be praying? You know I'm already praying for him, but I want to be able to pray specifically. It makes me feel just terrible that you're going through all this alone."

"Not exactly alone. I have some friends who are helping with Chesney and housecleaning and meals." She hesitated just a moment. "And God is especially near."

"He's close to the broken-hearted." A smile sounded in her mother's voice. "Do you need me there?"

Didn't everyone want their mother when times were hard? "Mom, I know you have so much to do this time of the year. Chesney and I are fine. But I did want to let you know so you can mail her gift. How's that project coming?"

"Great! In fact I'm almost finished. The swan idea was perfect. Wish I could be there to see her open it."

Heaviness fell once more. "I do, too, Mom. I do, too." She made a mental note to video Chesney opening the gift.

Once the phone call ended, Liv leaned back against the soft pillows and closed her eyes. Now to find the words to explain to Chesney that not only would she be doing Christmas without her father, but without the rest of her family as well. Was there any pain so great as breaking your child's heart?

An onslaught of tears erupted without warning. Liv didn't try to stop them. Instead she prayed through them, struggling to keep her focus on the Father rather than the emotional pain.

Later that afternoon, after church, lunch, and a nap, Chesney came into the room with a new box of crayons and coloring book. A smiling Deb wiggled fingers from the doorway, but then closed the door behind Chesney as Liv had requested.

Chesney crawled up on the bed beside Liv and cuddled up in the crook of her right arm. "Mommy, are you very, very sick?"

"No, sweetie, but the doctor's say I have to take special care of myself right now."

"How come?"

The big moment. This wasn't at all the way she'd hoped to break the news to Chesney. And part of her still hated to divulge the news in case the pregnancy ended with a miscarriage. But life had turned things around in a way that left her no choice. "I have some really good news, Chesney. Mommy and Daddy are having a baby brother or sister for you." She opted not to mention the potential for things to end badly.

Chesney's mouth widened to an "o". "You mean I'm going to be a big sister?"

Liv grinned and pulled her daughter into a sideways hug. "Yes. And I have no doubt that you'll be the best big sister ever."

Her daughter pulled back. "Does Daddy know?"

Liv shook her head sadly, wishing once more that she'd let Jeff know before his deployment. Maybe it would have provided him extra motivation to come home to them safely.

Chesney's features crumpled into darkness. "Has he called or sent you an email?"

"No, but I'm sure he will when he can."

Her little girl nodded, but the sad expression continued.

Inside her chest, the tug on Liv's heart was almost too much to bear. How could a four-year-old possibly understand how life so often came with not only broken pieces, but also unanswerable questions? Liv swallowed. There was still the news about the trip to deliver. "Chesney, because Mommy has to stay in bed to take care of the baby, we're not going to be able to spend Christmas with the rest of the family in Colorado."

To her great surprise, Chesney seemed to take the news in stride. She opened her coloring book and began coloring. "That's okay, Mommy. We can still have a good time together with just the two of us."

Through blinding tears, Liv once more turned her heart and mind toward God, thanking Him for His blessings in the midst of so many broken hopes and dreams, lifting a petition for safety for Jeff and their unborn child.

## Chapter Fifteen

One day stretched into the next to the point that Liv occasionally had to peek between the blinds to see if it were day or night. Her only consolation was her relationship to God and the contact with her friends and daughter. As each day passed with no word from Jeff, the fear grew so large inside that it was a constant battle to keep her trust in God stronger than the fear.

Thanksgiving Day arrived, with only Debbie joining them. Liv insisted on helping out with preparations as much as she could and on eating at the table. Afterwards they made the short drive to a nearby beach to let Chesney enjoy herself in the waves.

Liv laid back against her beach towel, the sand warm against her back, and glanced over at Debbie. "Thank you so much for this day, Debbie. It's been like a brilliant bright spot in the middle of tedious boredom."

"I don't know how you're doing it. I'd be ready to pull my hair out by now."

A laugh gurgled from her lips. "Trust me, I've been there."

Her friend pulled her knees to her chest, her expression contemplative. "The story you're telling Chesney. Do you really believe it?"

Goosebumps raised the hair on the back of Liv's neck, and in her thoughts, she sent an immediate prayer to heaven for guidance. "Yes, I do. Why do you ask?"

For a long minute Debbie didn't speak. "My parents always told me that the Bible was made up by men to brainwash people into doing what they want."

Liv shook her head. "That's not true, Deb. And I promise I'm not trying to brainwash you."

A slow chuckle sounded from Debbie, and she sent Liv a smile. "That's why I was so rude to you after Mike died."

Now it was Liv's turn to smile. "I'll bet you thought I would try to crawl in a window after you slammed the door in my face."

"The thought did cross my mind." She hesitated. "But this time of being around you and going to church with Marcy and Chesney has touched me in a way I can't fully explain. And the people at church have been wonderful. There's something wonderfully different about all of the Christians I've been around here lately." Debbie once more moved into quiet contemplation.

Liv inhaled deeply, another prayer winging its way from her heart. "Would you like to know more about becoming a Christian? It's really not that hard."

Though Debbie hesitated briefly, she nodded her head.

While Chesney continued to wade at the edge of the water, Liv explained the story of how man had failed and how Jesus had come to fix the problem.

The change in Debbie after that was nothing short of miraculous. Each week she took Chesney to church and eventually delivered the news that she had given her life to Christ. In addition to her friend's obvious peace and joy, her dreams of a food business grew with each passing day, prompting Liv to speak up.

"I'm sorry that my problems are delaying your dreams, Deb."

Debbie smiled graciously. "Please don't be. God is using this time in my life just as much as He is in yours."

Liv thought through the past few weeks. While it had been difficult, God was definitely at work. Mom still called, but the phone calls were often short rather than the lengthy calls they'd once enjoyed. Her mother obviously didn't want to tire her out. And in all fairness, it was a busy time of the year. With a large crew set to descend on her house for the trek to the cabin for Christmas, Mom had her hands full with the preparations.

Day after day passed, often in monotony. Though Liv tried hard not to descend into depression, it seemed to trail her like a shark after blood in the water. But when darkness attacked, she fought back with prayer and reading her Bible.

One day after school, Chesney once more bounded into the room. "Mommy, Miss Cindy says I really need to practice my part."

Liv frowned. They had practiced the short phrase to the point of perfection as soon as Chesney was given her part. "You knew it perfectly a few weeks ago."

"I know," Chesney revealed her dramatic flair with over-exaggerated hand motions, "I tried to tell Miss Cindy that, but she says I'm getting confused."

Liv smiled. "Okay. Tell you what. Why don't you say the line for me so I can see why Miss Cindy said that."

"Okay." She moved to the end of the bed and straightened her shoulders, an angelic expression on her face. "Glory to God in the highest, and on earth, pieces and good will to men."

Laughter rattled, but Liv quickly brought it under control at the tell-tale red that crept up her daughter's face. "You almost have it, but I can see why Miss Cindy said you were confused." While the occasional telling of the biggest story had been good for Chesney to grasp the overall message of the Bible, it had obviously interfered with her acting debut. "Remember when we talked about peace?"

"Yeah. We talked about it a lot. The rainbow was a promise of peace. The people God used to bring promises talked about peace, including the promise that the Fixer-- who is really Jesus--would be the Prince of Peace." Her daughter finished and gulped in a big breath of air, as though the recitation had spent every ounce of air in her lungs.

"Very good. Do you remember what the word "peace" really means?"

Chesney nodded. "It's being whole and complete, instead of broken in pieces."

A light bulb clicked on in Liv's mind. That's why Chesney was getting confused between peace and pieces. Not only did the words sound alike, but in a strange but wonderful way, they were intertwined with one another. She racked her brain to find a way to help Chesney remember. "Maybe it will help to think of it this way. In your line for the play, the angel is telling the world that Jesus came to bring glory to God and peace and good will to men. God didn't cause the pieces." She over-emphasized the "s" on the end of the word. "Man caused the pieces, but God brings peace."

A truly angelic smile took position on Chesney's face. "So then my line would be this. Glory to God in the highest, and on earth, peace and good will to men."

"Absolutely perfect." Another crisis averted.

Without warning, the doorbell rang. From the bed, Liv heard Debbie move to the front door. Though she couldn't make out what was being said, she heard not only Debbie's voice, but the voice of a man. Liv frowned. It was too early in the day for the mailman, UPS, or FedEx. Maybe it was news about Jeff?

She stood and made her way to the door. But just as she made a move to open it, Debbie swung it open instead. Her face was pale, making her eyes appear larger than normal. But it was the mixture of fear and sorrow Liv saw there that made her heart pound and the room spin out of control. She gripped the door frame. "What is it?"

"Some men from the Navy are here." The words fell from Debbie's lips in a hushed whisper.

Liv hunched over, her heart pounding. This couldn't be happening. *God help me be able to make it through this, whatever it is.* The answer to prayer came immediately, and Liv straightened to look Debbie in the eyes. "Take Chesney outside, and make sure she stays there please."

Debbie didn't answer, but nodded, her eyes still large in her wan face. Her friend motioned to Chesney. "C'mon, Ches. Let's go for a walk."

Praying for more strength, Liv released both the doorframe and a cleansing breath, then followed Debbie and Chesney toward the living room. While her friend and daughter exited by the back door, she moved to each man and shook their hands, fully aware of the sorrow and compassion in their eyes as she motioned to the couch. "Please have a seat." They did as she offered. She moved to one of the arm chairs and perched on the edge. "Okay. What is it?"

One of them lowered his head and twisted his white Navy cap in his hands, before looking up at her once more. "Ma'am, I'm sorry to inform you that your husband,

Lieutenant Jeffrey Tulley, is missing in action in Afghanistan."

*Sixteen*

A week later Liv rolled out of bed and traipsed to the bathroom mirror to stare at her reflection. Her eyes, red-rimmed and swollen from all the crying, stared back at her, lifeless. No surprise. Since the news, she'd slept or eaten very little, her heart continuously offering up prayers for Jeff's safety. In addition, she'd also scoured the internet for any news.

But news about the men missing in action was nowhere to be found. Instead she found report after report from military wife blogs about how much easier it was to hear that their husbands were dead than to learn they were missing in action.

The reason? No closure. Not knowing if they were dead or alive. And not much hope of any of those missing ever reappearing.

The depression she'd battled since Jeff's deployment had returned in full force. Though she still continued to read her Bible and pray, sometimes it seemed as though the walls of the bedroom closed in on her, covered with thick lead so her prayers couldn't make it past her prison walls.

A knock sounded at the door. "It's me, Liv. Can I come in?"

"Come on in, Deb. The door's unlocked." Liv called out the words and made her way back to the bed, holding her belly. By some miracle, her doctor's visits had given evidence that the baby inside her was alive and well. But how long would she be granted a reprieve if she continued on this path of depression, crying jags, and not eating?

Debbie entered with a tray and sat it on the hope chest at the end of the bed. She looked up at Liv with questions in her eyes. "How are you doing?"

"I'm falling to pieces, Deb, and I don't know how to stop it."

Her friend took a seat near the end of the bed and patted for Liv to come sit beside her. A compassionate gleam rested in her dark eyes. "I know this hard, Liv. You know that I've been where you are. I also know this is somewhat different, because Jeff is MIA." She hesitated, moved her gaze to the floor, and swallowed hard, before returning her earnest eyes once more to Liv. "I don't have all the answers, Liv, but I know this. There is a little girl who needs her Mommy strong and in one piece. If you can't do it for yourself, can you do it for her?" She hugged Liv's neck, sent one last sad smile, and then stepped out the door, closing it behind her.

For a minute Liv sat in total shock, a whole host of emotions washing through her, followed by an anger so strong it threatened to explode. How dare Deb lecture her about how she should feel and act, especially since she--of all people--understood the depth of her pain and hurt.

The doorbell rang, and Debbie's feet padded against the tile floors outside Liv's bedroom door. She straightened her spine. More bad news? She quickly donned her bath robe and slippers and stepped out into the hallway. She blinked against the bright light flooding through the front door.

A voice she recognized immediately as that of Marty Guthrie echoed across the room. "Hi, Liv."

Liv hurried toward her pottery teacher and the woman who stood beside him. She hugged his neck around the cardboard box he held in front of him. "So good to see you, Marty."

"Here let me set this box down so I can hug you properly and introduce you to my lovely bride." He stooped low to gingerly set the box on the tile floor, then raised to a standing position and enveloped her in a hearty hug. "I'm so sorry for all you're going through." He pulled away and motioned toward a gray-haired lady whose broad smile matched his own. "This is my wife, Helen."

To Liv's surprise, Helen also engulfed her in a hug. "So nice to meet you, Liv. Marty is always talking about how special you are, and he wanted to bring you a present."

Debbie stepped in at just the right moment. "Why don't we all have a seat, so Liv can open your gift?" She motioned them toward the couch, then delivered the box to the coffee table near where Liv sat.

Liv smiled at the Guthrie's. "Thank you so much. You really shouldn't have."

Marty grinned. "Oh, yes, we should have. And I can't wait to see your reaction."

She lifted one corner of one of the box flaps and then another, revealing several beautifully designed Christmas mugs, each different, but each with the same message carved into the bottom of each cup. "We're having a baby!" Immediate tears flooded her eyes, as she gently lifted one from the box. She brought trembling hands to her lips as she turned it from side to side. "They're beautiful." The words came out in a husky mess, but at least they sounded.

"I'm glad you like them, my dear." Marty's voice held the same huskiness. "When you called to postpone the rest of your lessons, I knew that I wanted to do this for you."

Debbie stepped over and helped her pull each large mug from the box and set them gently on the table, each one unique in design and color.

Helen gently cleared her throat. "What Marty hasn't told you is that we've been through something similar, but in a different line of work."

Questions erupted in Liv's chest and moved to her eyes. "What do you mean?"

Helen and Marty exchanged a smile before the elderly woman once more turned her gaze Liv's way. "Marty is a bi-vocational pastor, which by default makes me a bi-vocational pastor's wife." The couple shared a chuckle.

Liv let the words seep into her heart. On a very deep level, the similarities between her and Helen became apparent. Through no choice of her own--other than to marry a man in the military--she was a military wife by default. "I think I understand what you mean," she offered with a smile. "We both have an unspoken job description, one that is every bit as difficult and important as that of our husbands."

Helen nodded knowingly. "We're in the line of duty--and line of fire--just as much as they are. The wives and families of both pastors and soldiers are often overlooked and unappreciated. Add to that the loneliness--as well as being single parents for much of the time--and it can lead to major depression." She paused a minute her gaze fixed on some distance place beyond this one. "If you're like me, we feel the need to present an image of having it all together, when inside we're crumbling while we try to hold not only ourselves together, but also our family."

Tears slid unbidden and unchecked down Liv's face. "That's exactly how I feel." Beside her, Debbie nodded in agreement. "All that, in spite of not having a real job." She brought both hands up and used two fingers on each to etch quotation marks in the air and emphasized the word "real.". "It's the hardest job I've ever had--living with the unpredictability, and trying to deal not just with my anger and sorrow, but also my child's."

"And it's tough on your marriage." Marty joined the conversation, his voice revealing deep sorrow.

Helen scooted forward and placed her elbows on her knees, her fingers entwined and her gaze direct. "I don't know how you're coping at this particular moment, but if you don't mind I'd like to offer some advice."

Liv nodded her approval. "Please do. There are days when I'm grasping at straws in an attempt to hold on."

A wash of tears appeared in the old woman's eyes. "I understand those feelings more than you know. I went through a particularly bad time of depression and even suicidal thoughts, but I was afraid to seek psychological help." She craned her neck to look at Marty before turning back to Liv. "I was afraid it would affect Marty's job and make people look at me with even less favor than they already did."

A gasp fell from Liv's now-open lips. Similar thoughts had plagued her over the past week. It was as though God had sent Marty and Helen specifically on her behalf.

Helen continued. "First of all, please don't be afraid to seek professional help if you need it. Secondly, depend on God and His power. He knows what you're going through and will help you through it."

Marty stood, and Helen followed suit and took hold of his hand. "We need to go now, Liv, but if you need anything, night or day, please don't hesitate to give us a call. You still have my cell number, right?"

Liv nodded and rose to her feet. She moved to the couple, and embraced both of them at the same time. "Thank you both. You've helped more than you know."

After the couple left, Liv once more retreated to her room, this time to pray. Out of nowhere, an inexplicable peace flowed over her. Debbie had been right. Chesney needed her now more than ever. She lifted her eyes to the ceiling. *God, I don't know how to do this.*

*I am with you, child, and nothing is impossible for Me.*

The still small voice inside her head was distinct, and the words spoken were capital-T Truth as revealed in God's Word. Bolstered by power from beyond, Liv stood and opened the door, then picked up her breakfast tray and moved out to the living room.

Deb sat in her usual place, her fingers flying as she continued her latest crochet project. She looked up as Liv entered the room, laid down her work, and jumped to her feet. "Here. Let me help you with that." She grabbed the tray from Liv's hands. "Where do you want it?"

Liv nodded toward the glass-topped coffee table, the glass supported by a gnarled piece of driftwood Jeff had carried from the beach to the car at her request. She took a seat on the couch while Deb moved to the kitchen and re-warmed the food in the microwave. A minute later her friend returned and set the tray on the table.

A smile covered Liv's lips as she looked up at her friend. "Thank you, Debbie. I don't say it often enough, but--"

"I've already told you that I'm happy to do it." Debbie cocked her head to one side and gazed at Liv through narrowed eyes, encircled with fatigue. "You're better?"

Liv smiled again. "I think so. At first I was a little put out with you, but then I realized that it was the truth. I'm going to eat every bite of this breakfast, even if it kills me."

Deb's perfectly-arched eyebrows lifted in mock surprise. "Gee thanks for the testimonial about my cooking skills." The words came out with a sarcastic edge.

A laugh fell from Liv's mouth, the first one in days. She took a bite of the breakfast casserole. "You know good and well that's not what I meant." And she held true to her word, demolishing the food quickly.

That afternoon, when Darcy dropped Chesney off, Liv invited her daughter back to her bedroom. For the first time since the bad news, Liv truly looked at Chesney rather than staring through her as they sat cross-legged on the bed, facing one another. The news had worn on her daughter as well. Dark rings circled her little girl's eyes. "Chesney, I'm sorry Mommy hasn't been doing a better job of taking care of you."

Chesney's eyes, so much like her father's, took on a moist sheen. "It's okay, Mommy. I know the news about Daddy made you very sad. Me too."

Liv pulled her daughter into her arms and rocked her back and forth, a prayer of gratitude spilling from her heart for this blessed moment in time with her daughter. "I'm going to try to do better. We only have a few days until your play, and then just a few more days until Christmas. I want us to do our best to plan the most special Christmas ever." One that didn't downplay Jeff's MIA status, but one that celebrated his life with hope that they would one day see him again.

Her daughter pulled back, her chubby arms still resting around Liv's neck. A sweet smile rested between chubby cheeks. "I like that idea, Mommy. Want me to go get a pen and some paper so we can write down all our ideas?"

Liv leaned forward until her nose rested on her daughter's and gave her an Eskimo kiss. "Most definitely."

Chesney scrambled from the bed, disappeared for a moment, then returned with the promised pen and paper. She hurled herself up on the bed and scooted her bottom until her back rested against the headboard, obviously eager to move past the bad and focus instead on good news. Good news--like light in a dark place--always trumped the bad.

# PART 3

*Then rang the bells more loud and deep*
*God is not dead, nor doth He sleep*
*The wrong shall fail, the right prevail*
*With peace on earth, goodwill to men.*

## Seventeen

The night of Chesney's school play finally arrived. Though Liv stayed true to her promise to Chesney to do a better job, the devil seemed just as determined to attack her resolve. As she took a seat in between Debbie and Darcy near the front of the auditorium, a sudden wave of sorrow washed over her. If only Jeff were here to accompany her to Chesney's first performance.

Just as quickly, she fought back, her shoulders moving from their slump to an upright position. From the constant battle, she'd learned more and more to refuse the enemy so that he once more fled. This was Chesney's night, and she refused to let anything ruin it.

Beside her, Debbie set up the video camera and tripod. At least she'd be able to share this night with her family at a later time.

Within a few minutes the play began, a poignant reminder of the birth of her Savior, preciously portrayed by children. Though it was a special reminder of the reason for the season, the program was not without comical moments. Darcy's little girl played the part of Mary, and throughout the play she yanked her easily-distracted Joseph from place to place on the stage, eliciting hearty laughter from the audience.

Liv pressed her lips together, a sudden bout of nerves shimmying inside. In another minute or so, Chesney would take the stage with her one line. A line they had worked on over and over again. But since the news of Jeff's disappearance, no matter how many times they'd practiced at home, she always got it wrong. Would tonight be any different?

Beaming from ear to ear, Chesney and the rest of the angels bounced onto the stage, messy and out of file. Chesney sent Liv a smile and wave then turned to face the rest of the audience.

Liv swallowed hard, sending up prayers for her little girl, who looked particularly small and vulnerable tonight.

"Glory to God in the highest, and on earth...pieces..." Her daughter's voice, which had started strong, ebbed away in confusion. She looked over at Liv, her bottom lip a-quiver.

Liv nodded and smiled and mouthed the word "peace."

Chesney smiled and bravely faced the audience again, in spite of the snickers and chuckles sounding around the room. "I mean, glory to God in the highest, and on earth peace, good will toward men."

Tears slid down Liv's cheeks for the rest of the performance, her mind on the truth just spouted from the lips of her baby girl. Yes, the birth of this special God-baby into their mixed-up and messed-up world had fulfilled the angel's words in a way difficult to comprehend, but one that truly brought glory to God and boundless peace to human hearts. Even if the unthinkable had occurred. Even if Jeff no longer lived, she had the blessed hope that she'd one day see him again.

Later that night, back at home and once more obeying the doctor's order, Liv pulled Chesney into her quickly-disappearing lap. "Young lady, you did a marvelous job tonight. I'm so proud of you."

Chesney giggled and wiggled. "Thanks, Mommy. It was lots of fun, wasn't it? At first, I messed up my line, but then I looked at you and remembered."

Liv let the words sink in. An apt description of what God so often did for her. Whenever Liv focused on the storm, she forgot what she most needed to know. Only when she focused on Him did she gain the peace that only He could give. "So, let's work some more on our plans for Christmas Day. What do you want to eat for breakfast that day?"

"Pancakes!"

Liv grabbed the nearby notebook and pen and scribbled herself a note. Debbie would most likely make them Christmas-y and extra special. "And for lunch?"

"Macawoni and cheese pizza."

A chuckle gurgled from Liv's chest. "Well, we've had macawoni and cheese, but never on pizza."

"A.J.'s mom fixed it for him, and he told me about it."

"Ah, I see. I thought we'd open gifts right after breakfast. Does that sound like a good idea to you?"

Chesney's eyes grew wide with excitement. "Or we could wake up really, really early in the morning and open them before breakfast."

Liv grimaced at the thought, but relented inwardly. After all, this was a very special Christmas. "We'll see how it works out. Either one is fine with me. Then we'll play with your presents for awhile, call our family in Colorado, and eat lunch. Then a nap." She continued to write down their plans.

A horrified expression landed on Chesney's face. "No nap on Christmas!" She drawled out each syllable with her typical dramatic flair.

Liv laughed. "Okay, okay. Then what are we going to do after lunch?"

"Go to the beach, silly." Her daughter spoke the words matter-of-factly, then laid her head against Liv's shoulder.

As Liv snuggled even closer to her little girl, joy reigned in her heart. Yes, her daughter's plans for Christmas at the beach in no way matched her dream of a snowy-white Christmas in Colorado, surrounded by family. But even though life had changed her plans, this would be a wonderful Christmas in spite of it all. Not because of any plans they'd made, but because of the message of peace and hope delivered on that first Christmas in the gift of a baby boy who had come to deliver them from sin and death.

On Christmas Eve, Liv tucked Chesney--decked out in some Christmas pajamas Debbie had bought for her--under the covers and sat down on the bed next to her. "Tonight we get to the end of the story."

Chesney turned over to one side and looked up at Liv. "Remember when you told me that we were a part of the story?"

"Yes."

"Which part of the story are we in?"

"Well, in one way, we're in all of it, because we're all broken and need Jesus to fix us. But in another way, we're in the beginning of the end." Liv paused, a thought just then taking root in her brain. "Which is also the end of the beginning." Her heart filled with wonder at the way God had orchestrated His perfect plan.

"That may make to sense to you, but it doesn't make any sense to me." Chesney's voice held censure.

Liv laughed. "It will make more sense when you're older. I promise."

Chesney's face grew serious. "Isn't the world still broken, even after Jesus came?"

The thought sobered her. "Yes."

"Then He didn't really fix us, did He?"

Now Liv shook her head vehemently from side to side. "Just because we still live in a broken world doesn't mean that Jesus isn't fixing us. He fixes us from the inside out, and sometimes it's a slow process. And like the broken people we are, sometimes we don't realize how He's fixing us until we look back and see how He's glued us back together." Liv thought back over the past few months. Yes, the Fixer had been evident in her heart and life during the most difficult of times. Had brought a peace she'd never expected in the midst of her brokenness. He'd also changed Debbie in such a way that still astounded her.

"Like me learning to be nice to A.J. when he's mean to me?"

"Exactly like that." Liv opened her Bible. "The Fixer--Jesus--will one day come back to earth to do away with the snake and his lies forever. When He comes back, He'll make everything brand new."

A contented sigh fell from Chesney's lips. "That will be perfectly wonderful." She paused. "But why doesn't He go ahead and come back now?"

"Because He wants more people to recognize their broken pieces and turn to Him to fix them. So until the end of the story--which is the beginning of a brand new story--there will still be broken pieces on earth. But when Jesus comes again, He'll take away all the broken pieces and mess-ups and death and sickness--"

"--and crying and war and daddies being gone for a very, very, very long time." Chesney's eyes flooded with tears. "I do want more people to get fixed, but it would be really wonderful if Jesus came back right now."

Liv hugged her daughter close. Yes, that would be wonderful, and something she longed for as well. She released a happy sigh. But for now, it was enough that He was in control and operating on His time-table to restore everything to what He'd originally intended when He'd created the world in the first place.

# Eighteen

Christmas Day dawned bright and beautiful, with flawless blue skies and a warm southerly breeze. Liv sipped her morning cup of coffee. Chesney would be awake soon and eager to open presents. From her perch at the dining room table, she gazed out the sliding glass doors at the lovely day. Her thoughts took wing, and she remembered how different this day would have been had things gone according to her plan.

If life had turned out her way, she and Jeff and Chesney would be waking up at the mountain cabin in Colorado with all their siblings and both sets of parents. They would dress in warm Christmas sweaters and snow boots, toasting one another with the mugs she'd made, now full of hot cider or cocoa in front of a blazing fire and a Christmas tree bedecked in white lights and heirloom ornaments--one that scraped the ceiling.

But life had different plans. Plans that involved a new baby, a changed friend, and personal transformation from fear to peace.

Liv peered over to the living room, amazed at the transformation that had taken place--not only in human lives, but in their home in sunny Pensacola, Florida. She and Debbie had worked until midnight to turn their tropical location living room into a winter wonderland for Chesney. Though the dangling snowflakes and piles of cotton batting at least resembled what she'd hoped for, it also set off a longing in her heart.

*Stop it, Liv.* She gave her head a shake to toss aside the unhelpful thoughts. Thinking about the "what might have been's" wasn't going to cut it. She squared her shoulders and breathed deeply. Instead she would focus on what was. It was a beautiful day to share with her daughter, unborn child, and friend. Though there was still the question of whether Jeff would ever come home to them, she could still rest in the beauty of God's peace in spite of it all.

"Mommy! Mommy!" Chesney's voice sounded, followed by footsteps pitter-pattering against the tile floors. "It's Christmas! The day Baby Jesus was born!" She rounded the corner and threw herself into her mother's arms, then peered around at the wintry scene, her mouth agape. "Wow!"

"It certainly is." Liv smiled at her daughter. "And as you can see, we're going to celebrate it in style. Debbie's making those Christmas pancakes you wanted, and then we'll take the Happy Birthday Jesus cake we made yesterday to the nursing home."

Chesney took over the retelling of the list they had finally agreed upon. "Then we'll open Christmas presents and go to the beach for a picnic lunch with macawoni and cheese pizza."

"Exacalacaly."

Chesney let out a overly-dramatic and forced belly laugh.

Debbie appeared in the opening to the kitchen, a plate of strawberry pancakes topped with whipped cream in her hands. "Merry Christmas!"

Later that morning, after the pancakes and delivery of the "Happy Birthday, Jesus" cake to a nearby nursing home, Chesney eagerly ripped into the biggest package, one that Jeff had instructed her to buy before they'd lost contact.

"My toy Jeep! Thank you, Mommy."

"It was your Daddy's idea. After I told him that you wanted one, he asked me to get it as your gift from us."

Chesney came to an abrupt halt. "I wish Daddy could call us. It's Christmas."

"I know, Ches." Liv tousled her daughter's red curls. "But let's not be sad on Christmas." At least as much as they could manage.

Chesney went back to work, removing every last shred of paper from her Jeep. "Don't forget to take your cell phone to the beach, just in case he calls while we're there."

Her heart caught in her throat, but she managed a croaky "I won't."

Her daughter continued to open packages from aunts, uncles, cousins, and grandparents. The last one she opened was the gift Mom had made. It had arrived on the UPS truck only yesterday. As soon as the package was open, Chesney squealed with glee. "A red Santa dress. And look, it has swans on the bottom of it! Just what I wanted!" She immediately stood, disrobed, and donned the dress, along with the matching red Santa hat with jingle bells sewn on. "I'm wearing it to the beach."

"You'll burn up in that dress on the beach." Debbie half-laughed the words, and Liv nodded in agreement.

"That's okay. I don't care."

Liv started to protest, but decided against it. It was Christmas, and special for reasons Liv would never have imagined. "Okay, but we'll take your swimsuit in case you change your mind."

Chelsea delved to the back of the gifts still under the tree. "Here's my present for you, Mommy."

"You got me a gift?" Liv took the messily-wrapped present from her daughter's hands, and looked over at Debbie.

Her friend shrugged to indicate she had nothing to do with it.

"No, I made you a gift. Miss Cindy helped me."

Liv reached out and gave her daughter a hug, touched by the simple gesture and once more marveling that her little girl was growing up so quickly. "Thank you, Chesney."

"I hope you like it."

"I can guarantee you that I will, because you made it." Liv tore into the paper and opened the box. Pushing aside white tissue paper, she retrieved a conch shell from within the box. And not just any conch shell, but one that had been broken and carefully glued back together. Her eyes swam with tears as she looked up at Chesney. "It's beautiful."

"I found it on the beach all broken, but I picked up all the pieces and put them in my beach bag. Miss Cindy helped me at school. I told her I thought you would like it because of the story you told me. She asked about the story, so I told her about broken people and the Fixer. She even started crying."

Liv pulled her daughter into a bear hug, tears coursing down her cheeks, amazed at how the good news could spread, even through the lips of a child. "It's the perfect Christmas gift for this particular Christmas, Chesney. I'll cherish it always." Cherish it not only as a gift from her daughter, but a reminder that life was often like that seashell--made for a distinct purpose--but sometimes broken against the shorelines of an imperfect and strife-filled world. But like the glued-together shell, the Prince of Peace brought peace and wholeness to those He fixed.

Later that day, their macaroni and cheese pizza in tow, Liv, Chesney, and Debbie made their way to the beach, the sea-salty breeze tugging at their hair. Chesney proudly wore her heavy red-velvet Christmas dress and matching hat, despite the warm day.

They reached an acceptable spot on the beach and spread out their beach blanket. Liv quickly kicked off her shoes and dug her toes into the powdered-sugar sand warmed by heat from the sun. Her shoulders relaxed. Yes, this had been a great Christmas.

Several minutes later, after they finished off the special macawoni and cheese pizza Debbie had insisted on making. Liv glanced over at her friend. "The pizza was wonderful. Remind me to have it more often."

Debbie laughed and pulled her knees up to her chest, peering out to the ocean, where Chesney now waded, once more in search of broken shells. "It was, wasn't it? Trust me, I'm just as surprised as you are."

"Another item to add to your menu when you open your restaurant."

Her friend yanked her arm up to peer at her watch. "That reminds me, I have a phone call to make. Will you be okay here by yourself for a few minutes while I run up to the car to make the call? It's so windy down here, I'm not sure I'll be heard unless I'm sitting in the car."

"Of course. Go ahead."

As Debbie made her way up the sandy road toward the nearby parking lot, Liv peered out to where Chesney waded at the edge of the waves, the water lapping her pudgy feet. Their carefully-made plans had kept them all from dwelling on darkness. But as she sat alone, a sorrow so deep that it hindered her ability to breathe, washed over her like a giant wave. *Oh God, I'm so grateful for this day, but please help me not to ruin it for Chesney and Debbie by being sad and depressed.*

Without warning, her daughter straightened and put a hand over her eyes to shield them from the sun as she peered down the beach.

Liv followed the direction of her gaze. On the empty shore walked a solitary figure. As the person drew closer, Liv rose to her feet, not quite believing her eyes. Was she just dreaming? She squeezed her eyes shut for several seconds, willing the mirage away, but when she opened them, the figure was still there. Only now the person ran full-force, growing ever bigger and more certain with each second.

Against doctor's orders, Liv found her own feet running toward the figure, Chesney following suit at water's edge. "Jeff! Is that you?"

In a heartbeat she rested in his arms, Chesney engulfed in the same familiar hug, tears flowing freely among all of them. When at last the tears were somewhat controlled, Liv pulled back. "How are you here?"

Jeff, his own face damp, grinned. "It's a long story."

"I'd be content with the condensed version." Even though all that really mattered that he was here, safe and sound. And alive.

He laughed out loud and plopped a kiss on Chesney's giggling mouth, then followed it with another kiss on her own lips. "The short story is that our plane had to make an emergency landing behind enemy lines. We were captured and held in some caves in the Afghan mountains. They sent a group to rescue us, and then after de-briefing, sent us home. I called Darcy so I could surprise you. She orchestrated everything with Debbie's help."

Liv shook her head, flabbergasted. How had the worst possible news resulted in the best possible news? The answer came immediately, singing and winging through her head and heart. Only God could work this kind of miracle. Only He could take broken lives, hopes, and dreams, and recreate them into masterpieces.

Later that night, after Chesney was in bed, Jeff pulled Liv to him and kissed her soundly beneath the mistletoe she'd hung with absolutely no hope of it being put to use.

A minute later, the kiss ended, but Liv snuggled closer to her husband, enraptured by the sound of his heart thumping within his chest. *Oh, God, thank You for this gift. Thank You for bringing him home to us.* She pulled back, her arms still wrapped around his neck, and peered happily into his eyes. "I have a gift I want you to open."

He grimaced. "I'm sorry, Liv. There just wasn't time for me to get you anything."

"Are you kidding me? I got exactly what I wanted for Christmas." Liv planted a kiss on Jeff's mouth, released her grasp on his neck, and moved to the back side of the tree. She retrieved the gift she'd wrapped, not knowing if it would ever be unwrapped, handed it to him and watched as he unwrapped it.

A few seconds later, he pulled the mug from its box and tissue paper, then looked at her quizzically.

"Look inside."

Her husband held the mug toward the lights of the Christmas tree in the semi-darkened room. The smile on his lips disappeared, and he yanked his head her way, his jaw gaping. "But, I thought--"

"Me, too, but God apparently had other plans."

In two steps, she was back in his arms as the tears once more flowed freely. He nuzzled her neck, and pulled her into a seated position in his lap on the sofa. "Why didn't you tell me sooner?"

Heart in her throat, Liv relayed the story about how her anger had kept her from telling him, but how God had used the brokenness she'd experienced to draw her closer to Him. "I'm not proud of how I behaved, Jeff. Will you forgive me?"

"Of course." He shook his head in amazement. "But once we get some sleep, I want the whole story."

The whole story? If she'd learned anything over the months of sharing the story with Chesney, it was that the whole story was much bigger than both of them. Liv rested her head against his chest and once more reveled in the sound of the beat of his heart. A moment of complete awe enveloped her. How miraculous that each of their stories found its place--in spite of broken pieces--intertwined in the biggest story of all time.

*Then ringing singing on its way*
*The world revolved from night to day*
*A voice, a chime, a chant sublime*
*Of peace on earth, goodwill to men.*

127

## About the Author

A native Texas gal, Cathy currently resides in the small Texas town where she grew up. When she's not writing you'll find her digging in the dirt, rummaging through thrift stores, or up to her elbows in yet another home improvement project. In addition to the Miller's Creek novels, Cathy has also written novellas, Bible studies and devotional books.

To learn more about Cathy and her books, visit her website at www.CathyBryantBooks.wordpress.com. Besides her website, Cathy also loves to connect with readers on social media.

Facebook page: /Cathy.Bryant.Author
Twitter: @Cathy_Bryant
Pinterest: cathyjbryant

*Dear friends,*

*I've heard it said that only two things are guaranteed in this life--taxes and our own mortality. But I beg to differ and ask permission to add a third item for your consideration. I believe that this earthly life also carries with it broken pieces. None of us are immune. Into each of our lives thunder those life-storms that steal our breath away and leave our broken pieces in their wake.*

*But there is a fourth item available for those who--in the midst of the broken pieces--turn to Jesus.*

*He truly is the Prince of Peace and our pieces. Only He can mend us and make us new.*

*My prayer for each of us as we enjoy this blessed Christmas season is that we'll be extra aware of His Presence and that we'll gladly surrender our broken pieces to Him.*

**An especially-blessed and Merry Christmas to you and yours,**
Cathy

*P.S. I hope you enjoyed* **Pieces on Earth** *as much as I enjoyed writing it. More importantly, I hope the message of God's astounding peace filled each of our hearts with the peace that only God can give. If you enjoyed the story, would mind leaving your honest review in places like Amazon, Barnes & Noble, and Goodreads. This not only helps me, but other readers. Thank you.*

## Other Miller's Creek Novels

### *Texas Roads*

*A hurting seeker longs for home in a back roads country town until malicious rumors propel her down a road she never expected to travel.*

### *A Path Less Traveled*

*A widow with shaken faith is determined to blaze a trail for herself and her traumatized son, but must regain her faith to take a path less traveled.*

### *The Way of Grace*

*Can a fallen perfectionist--especially in the face of life-altering circumstances--bestow on others the grace God has lavished on her?*

### *Pilgrimage of Promise*

*A dusty stack of unopened love letters forces a betrayed woman to revisit a part of her past she'd rather leave buried—especially when confronted with her husband's impending death.*

### *A Bridge Unbroken*

*A frightened runaway co-inherits a farm with the man responsible for the scars on her heart. Can the two move past old wounds and grudges to build a bridge unbroken?*

### *Crossroads*

*A soldier wages war for the souls of a bitter prodigal and her terminally-ill little girl.*

## Miller's Creek Collection 1
*Now the first three books of the beloved Miller's Creek novels are available in a bundled digital edition. Enjoy Texas country romance and romantic suspense with spiritual themes of finding home, regaining faith, and demonstrating grace.*

## Miller's Creek Collection 2
*This second trilogy collection of faith-based stories, novels 4-6 in the beloved Miller's Creek novels by Christian author Cathy Bryant shares the messages of God's unfailing promises, our need to give and receive forgiveness, and being prepared to defend our faith.*

## Other Books by Cathy Bryant

### The Fragrance of Crushed Violets: Forgiving the Inexcusable
*A Bible Study About Forgiveness*
*Companion to A BRIDGE UNBROKEN*

*How do we handle it when the assault of another is personal, public, deep, unjust, unfair, and unfounded? Take it one step further. How do we deal with meaningless acts of destruction and death such as the Twin Towers incident or a school shooting, especially when the offender shows no remorse? This Bible study explores these questions and more as we examine forgiveness through the eyes of faith.*

## Believe & Know
### A Bible Study About Defending The Faith
### Companion to CROSSROADS

*Each human being, on their journey and search for truth, must at some point reflect on their life and answer important questions. Why am I here? Is there life beyond life as I now know it? How did the universe and man come into existence, and how does the answer affect me? This book addresses the hard questions and decisions that accompany the search for truth. It was written with three types of readers in mind: those who struggle with faith, those who profess faith in the unseen, but find it difficult to live out; and those whose faith is strong, but who need information to better answer the tough questions of skeptics.*

## Miller's Creek Forgiveness Collection
*Snatch up both A BRIDGE UNBROKEN and its companion Bible study on forgiveness (THE FRAGRANCE OF CRUSHED VIOLETS) in this special digital collection for one low price.*

## CROSSROADS

*Bonus chapter from the sixth stand-alone book in the Miller's Creek novels*

Out of pure reflex, Mara stiffened her right leg and stomped the brake pedal to the floor, tires a-screech against the asphalt as the undeniable odor of burning rubber reached her nose. She gritted her teeth, her breath in rapid spurts, and yanked the steering wheel hard to the right. Her clenched jaw relaxed just enough to spout words that had conglomerated in her sour-tasting mouth. "Please don't let me run over this stupid animal."

Just who did she think she was talking to? She shrugged. No one. Nothing. Thin air. Her salty lips had simply taken on a life of their own without permission. The new-to-her Cadillac Escalade finally bounced to a halt, and her body echoed the move.

Once her brain stopped sloshing around in her skull, Mara jerked her head to the left to see the armadillo-- almost the exact color of the pavement--waddle nonchalantly through the bar ditch and under a barbed- wire fence. The squatty body animal disappeared behind the thick growth of mesquite, cedar, live oak, and clumps of prickly pear cactus.

She brought a trembling hand to her throat and willed her shallow breaths and racing heart to a slower pace. Yet another thing to adjust to in the small back-roads country town of Miller's Creek.

Critters.

She sniffed at the still form of a black and white pile of fur in the road next to her. The rancid smell of squished skunk--who hadn't fared as well as the armadillo--stung Mara's nostrils, bringing tears to her eyes and wrinkles to the bridge of her nose.

Yeah, she'd experienced rural Texas before, but it had been years, her childhood a murky fog that took up residence in the distant recesses of her mind. Had she blocked out painful memories by imprisoning that part of her life behind lock and key?

Her gaze flitted to the dashboard clock, and set her into instant motion. "Oh no. Please no." This couldn't be happening. Not on a day when she actually had a prospective customer to help pay her bills and feed her family. She quickly released the brake and pressed the accelerator, the horses beneath the hood rapidly roaring to life and charging down the road.

Now she'd never make her four o'clock appointment with Carter Callahan. Of course it wasn't as though he'd given her ample time to find him a house. He'd called right before lunch and said he needed a house, and then promptly ended the call with some mumbled excuse about being on duty and without giving any details as to what kind of property he wanted. Fearful that as a policeman on duty he had more important matters to deal with, she'd opted not to call back. Instead she'd spent her afternoon viewing possible properties to show him.

Mara quelled her anxious thoughts with a sip of warm and non-fizzy Diet Coke, the flat and tepid liquid leaving the after-taste of artificial sweetener on her tongue. She made a face and clunked the can into the console drink holder. Was this her third one today, or her fourth? She inched the accelerator closer to the floor.

At five minutes after four, she pulled up outside the building she'd leased from Otis Thacker, more proof of the number one rule in real estate. Location, location, location. Nestled between recently-renovated turn-of-the-century buildings on the picturesque town square, and boasting creamy-white Austin stone, cinnamon-colored cedar posts, and rustic tin roof, the place screamed central Texas. The perfect store front for her new business, one that needed to turn a profit. And soon.

The unlocked seat belt slipped from her fingers and clanked against the door as she scooped up her purse and manila file folders. She climbed from the SUV, glanced down the thick slab of elevated sidewalk, and slammed the door.

No sign of Carter Callahan.

Had he come and left already? More than a little disgruntled at the missed appointment and chance at a potential sale, she trudged to the door. At some point, she'd just have to bite the bullet and hire a receptionist for times like these, but with money so tight, it was hard to justify the expense.

Mara moved across the large open space dotted with office furniture she'd purchased at a hotel sale, and into her office, where she plunked the folders atop the granite-looking counter top behind her desk. Next she slung her suit-case-sized purse--an ironic microcosm of her hectic life--onto the desk, contents spilling from inside. She snatched up her eBay iPhone, and fingers ablaze, punched in Carter's number, scrawled on a nearby pink sticky-note.

The electronic beeps from her phone bounced off walls and oak floors.

"Police department."

A disgusted sigh whooshed from her lungs. Not exactly who she'd hoped for. "Ernie? Is that you?"

"Yep. Mara?"

"Yeah, it's me. Sorry to bother you. I'm trying to reach Carter Callahan. Is he there by any chance?"

"Nope. Just left. Said he had a couple of errands to run."

Hope ignited in her chest. Good. Hopefully he hadn't forgotten her. But how much longer would she have to wait? "Did he happen to say what errands?"

"Something about paying the electric bill and stopping by the post office to mail a package."

Her spirits instantly deflated. Okay, so maybe he had forgotten her. "If you happen to see him would you have him call me at the office?"

"Okey-dokey." Ernie drawled out the words, Texas-style, right before the line went dead.

Mara eyed the clock. How could he be so inconsiderate of her time? Yeah, she'd been late too, but she'd dropped other things to get there as soon as possible. As the second hand of the clock ticked off the ever-fleeting time, she ticked off her to-do list for the rest of the day. Pick up Ashton from the daycare by five. Cram down a few bites of leftover goulash before the Miller's Creek Talent Show rehearsal. Follow up on a few leads and hopefully line up showings for the next day. The rehearsal should be over by seven or seven-thirty, which would give them ample time for outdoor play, Kindergarten homework, and Ashton's nightly bath before story time and bed. Then...

Her thoughts strayed to yet another evening by herself, and unexpected loneliness landed like a lead blanket. A solitary sigh escaped. She'd known being a single parent would be difficult. Had known moving to a new place to start a business would be challenging. But one thing she hadn't taken into consideration was the mind-numbing isolation of interminable nights.

Mara gave her head a gentle shake, careful not to dislodge the rock hard hair-sprayed bun she'd crafted early that morning to keep her naturally curly hair in check.

*Snap out of it, Mara.*

Life in Miller's Creek was certainly better than living with the man who no longer loved her. She rubbed the bridge of her nose. No use dwelling on it. Giving in to the Black Abyss would be counter-productive and foolish. She had to find a way to distract herself from the depression that threatened to swallow her alive.

From outside her office the front door bell buzzed, announcing a visitor. Carter hopefully?

Mara stood, wiped sweaty palms against her polyester skirt, pasted on her most brilliant business smile, and moved to the main office, her high heels clicking against the wooden floors. She extended a hand toward the larger-than-life man silhouetted against the backdrop of front plate-glass windows. "Hi, Carter. I'm Mara Hedwig. So nice to finally meet you in person."

He engulfed her hand with both his bear paws, an equally large grin splayed on his scruffy-but-handsome face. "Hey, Mara. Sorry I'm late. Blame it on my crazy life."

*His crazy life?* He had no idea what crazy was until he'd experienced just a fraction of the *la vida loca* she lived. She bit back a retort. "Well, we'd best get a move on it if we're going to get to these houses I've lined up for us to see. Let me get my things." She clicked back to her office, sipped a quick drink of her fourth Diet Coke, and grabbed the folder with Carter's name scribbled on it, along with her purse and keys.

A few minutes later they stood outside on the sidewalk in the humid-hot dog days of a sizzling Texas summer as Mara locked up the building and moved toward the driver's side of the Escalade. "We'll go in my car."

Carter released a low whistle as he folded his over-sized frame into the leather passenger seat. "Business must be good."

Not exactly. But definitely the impression she wanted to make, and the reason she'd purchased this way-too-expensive gas-guzzler. According to the latest real estate how-to book she'd read, potential clients were drawn to perceived success.

Rather than responding to his comment, Mara smiled politely, clicked her seat belt into position, and cranked the engine to a gentle purr. Two minutes later they pulled up outside the first place, a tiny frame house within easy walking distance of the town square and Miller's Creek police department. She glanced at her expensive-looking knock-off wristwatch as she parked. If she could get him in and out of here in five to ten minutes, she might just be able to keep her five o'clock deadline. "Here's our first listing. A one-bedroom, one-bath, detached home with a carport."

Carter's dark eyebrows met in the middle. Not a positive sign. "Don't think this one will be big enough for me and my daughter."

"Daughter?" Mara's frozen smile melted from within, her stomach churning up bitter acid in response. "Sorry. You didn't really give me a chance in our phone conversation to find out what you were looking for. I assumed you wanted a place for just you."

He shook his head. "No. My teenage daughter Chloe lives with me now. The apartment complex we're in isn't ideal, and we're beyond over-crowded." His gaze focused somewhere down the street. "Didn't know one teen-age girl came with so much paraphernalia."

"Oh." Mara pursed her lips, her brain clicking through options like a line of people at a Six Flags turnstile. "Well, if this one's too small, we won't even bother with it." At least that would save some time. She opened his client folder and whisked through a few papers, quickly spotting the information she sought. "The next house I lined up is a two-bedroom, two-bath, probably more suited to what you're looking for."

Carter grinned to reveal even white teeth that practically sparkled against his tanned skin. He scratched his chin whiskers. "Sounds more like it. Definitely don't enjoy sharing a bathroom with a teen-aged female. Don't get a whole lot of mirror time anymore."

Mara laughed as she pulled away from the curb. Like he needed mirror time. "Just so you know, I'm pretty sure the teenage girl doesn't like sharing a bathroom anymore than you do."

His charming smile and deep chuckle set off a strange twist in her stomach.

139

Okay, back to business. Now would be a great time to ask a few questions. "Other than the two beds and two baths, is there anything else you're looking for?"

"Not really. All comes down to space and budget."

Mara released a semi-silent sigh of relief as she turned a corner. Good. He'd brought up the money issue first. "How much are you wanting to spend?"

"I'd like to keep it close to what I'm paying for the apartment. Seven hundred a month."

Quick calculations erupted in her head. Thirty year mortgage, twenty percent down. He'd be able to afford over a hundred thousand with no problem. A smile flickered inside and worked its way to her face. Which meant that after splitting realtor's fees with the listing agent she could plop at least three grand in her almost-depleted bank account. "I'm sure we can find you something very nice for that amount."

Carter's eyes widened. "Really?" His tone held shocked surprise.

"Really." Mara pulled up in front of house two and grimaced inwardly. Ugh. The old bungalow had definitely seen better days and was well under what he could afford. But this wasn't a good way to impress a new client. Oh well, at least she could see what he liked and disliked about the place, info that would make further research all the easier.

They stepped from the vehicle at the same time and made their way down the narrow and crumbling sidewalk to a small stoop of a porch. Mara retrieved the key from the lock box with fumbling fingers, painfully aware that Carter used the time to scan the declining neighborhood. Rats!

Yet another minus to add to his list of negatives about the place.

He stepped up beside her. "Well-established neighborhood. I like that. We don't get too many calls from this part of town. I like that even better. Mostly older folks around here."

Mara swung the front door open, filing his comments within compartments in her brain to add to her files later that night. "So you'd rather have friends for your daughter in the neighborhood?"

Carter's face took on an indiscernible look. "Not really, but I guess it depends on the friends." His tone held a trace of sarcasm.

Her eyebrows climbed despite her attempt to keep them down. Over-protective dad? Poor Chloe. Mara held one hand toward the tiny living space. "This, of course, would be your main living area, and it leads to an eat-in kitchen."

Carter sauntered across the stained and tattered carpet to the kitchen, his eyes roving over every square inch. "More outdated than what we're used to, but it'll do."

This time Mara locked her eyebrows in down position and forced her lips into a placid smile. Hello. Could he not see how horrible this kitchen was? No telling how many layers of grease coated the mustard-gold stove or what kind of creepy-crawlies lurked in darkened crevices. Not to mention the musty smell. Yeah, time to move on. "The bedrooms are this way." She took off down the hallway, then flattened herself against the wall to allow his brawny build to pass by. "The first doorway on the left is the second bedroom, and across the hall is a bath." If you could call the postage-stamp-sized bath a room.

He poked his head around the door frame of the pink-tiled bathroom and grimaced. "It's a bit tight for me. And pink's definitely not my color." His gaze roved to the low shower head. "I'd have to chop myself off at the knees to fit under that thing."

"This isn't the master bath. Maybe it's more your size."

He scratched his head. "Maybe, but I'll probably give Chloe the master. Trust me, she'll need it for all her stuff."

Mara traipsed to the master bedroom with the en suite bath. It wasn't much bigger than the first.

Though Carter didn't speak, she could tell by the turn of his lips that it wasn't to his taste. "How big is the back yard?"

"Fairly large, actually." She moved to a window and peered out the dust-covered blinds, then stepped aside for him to look. "It would give you plenty of space for entertaining."

One side of his upper lip curled. "Yuck. Yard work. And just so you know, I'm not much into entertaining. Just need enough space for the dogs."

She should've seen that one coming. He was definitely the dog type, which meant he definitely wasn't her type. Not that she was on the market anyway. "So you'd rather have a small yard?"

"Definitely. Don't mind yard work, but my free time is next to nil."

She nodded. "I totally understand." Understatement of the millennium. "Are you interested in this one at all?"

"Maybe. How much?"

"Well under budget at fifty-five."

A puzzled expression clouded his face. "Fifty-five?"

"Yes. Fifty-five thousand. Is that a problem? I'm sure you're pre-qualified for more than that." She hesitated. "Aren't you?"

His chuckle broke lose along with a sheepish grin. "Uh, I'm looking for a place to rent. Not to buy."

Steam built in her ears and threatened to explode out the top of her head. Well. He could've at least asked if there were rentals available when he called. All this time she'd assumed he was looking to buy. And she'd make next to nothing on finding him a rent house. Her smile slipped, but she ducked her head and headed to the front door without comment.

Once she'd turned off the lights and secured the house, Mara hurried to the SUV with Carter right behind. She inched the speedometer needle a hair above the speed limit as they made their way to the final house for the day. What was the best way to broach this subject of rental houses? She cleared her throat and assumed her best business voice. "You should know that the next house I have lined up is also for sale. Sorry about the miscommunication, but my business revolves around sales. Since you didn't mention rent houses, I assumed you wanted to purchase a home."

"You don't do rentals?"

She sent an apologetic smile. "Not at this point. And quite honestly, I think you might have trouble locating a rent house in a place the size of Miller's Creek. Most people only rent when they become desperate and can't sell their house." She peered in the rear view mirror as she slowed to a stop at an intersection.

A heavy sigh sounded from the other side of the car. "Problem is, I don't wanna buy. Chloe graduates next May, so I'll more than likely move to a bigger place where there's better pay. Need the extra income to send her to college."

Mara pulled the SUV onto the shoulder of the road and braked to a stop, then turned to look at him squarely. Might as well end this now so she could get on with the next portion of her day's crazy agenda. "So you don't want to see the next house?" She sent a quick glance to the dashboard clock. Hopefully he'd take the hint. Already she was late in picking Ashton up from the daycare.

"You need to be somewhere?" One dark eyebrow cocked upward, reminding her of the furry caterpillars that had already made their appearance in the trees outside her front door.

"Not if you're interested in buying this house." Sometimes bluntness was the only thing that got through to this kind of guy. She bit back the urge to tell him how he'd wasted her time. Time she wanted--and needed--to spend with her daughter.

He considered her words. "I have an idea. Let's swing through the Dairy Queen drive-thru so I can pick up a burger. I missed lunch, and my stomach thinks my throat's been cut. Then we'll hop on over to that other house. Maybe I just need to bite the bullet and buy a house."

His first words had generated an automated response of 'you've-got-to-be-kidding-me' in her brain. Had he not followed them with the hint of a possible purchase, she'd be dropping him off and pronto. She gulped deep breaths of air to squelch her growing frustration at his devil-may-care attitude. Okay, she could do this. After all, she was a mom, right? She'd grab some chicken nuggets for Ashton at the DQ to save time. Not the healthiest meal, but on their tight time frame it would have to work. Another plan hatched in her mind, and a triumphant grin landed on her lips. And the daycare was on the way to the next house, so she might as well pick Ashton up on the way.

Ten minutes later, the SUV now flooded with the smell of fast food--Mara pulled back onto the highway as Carter noisily dug around in the bulging white paper sack. He pulled out a small white box with red lettering and sat it on the console between them. "Here's your chicken nuggets."

"Oh, they're not for me. They're for my daughter. Her day care is on the way to the next house, so I'm going to pick her up. Do you mind?"

"Not at all." He spoke the words through swollen cheeks, much like a squirrel during nut season, his voice muffled by the wad of burger in his mouth. As they pulled up outside the daycare, Carter stuffed in the last morsel of his double-patty burger with bacon and cheese and licked his fingers with a slurping sound.

Mara ignored his caveman manners, put the vehicle in park, and killed the engine.

Carter lifted his gaze. "Hey, this is Mama Beth's daycare."

"Yes, it is."

"Mind if I go in with you?"

A wild chase of panic and frustration erupted inside. Would they ever get through this house showing? "Sure. Why not?" A dead-pan tone crept into her voice as she exited the Escalade and hurried to the front door to punch in her security code. A second later they entered the sprawling ranch house which had been converted to a

145

daycare, each room set up for various activities especially geared to preschool-aged children.

Dani Miller rounded the corner of the hallway, a baby on her right hip. "Hi, Mara." Then she looked past her to Carter. "Well, what are you doing here, big guy?" She eased around Mara to give him a sideways hug.

Carter laughed, a rich melodious sound that echoed through the space. "Mara's showing me some houses, but wanted to stop and pick up her daughter. So I thought I'd come in and say hi."

A strange calculating twinkle developed behind Dani's big blue eyes. "Ah, I see. Y'all follow me. The kids are outside."

A minute later they stood in the fenced-in play yard beside Mama Beth, who looked out over the handful of children yet to be picked up. Ashton leaned against the elderly woman's right side.

Mara knelt in front of her daughter and enveloped her in a hug. "Guess what I have waiting for you in the car?"

Ashton smiled a tiny smile, the fatigue of the day resting in her eyes. "What?"

"Chicken nuggets from Dairy Queen."

Instead of being happy about the uncommon treat of fast food chicken nuggets, her daughter pointed to Carter. "Who's that?"

Mara latched on to her daughter's finger and pulled downward, then rose to her feet. "Don't point, sweetie. It's impolite. I'm showing Mr. Callahan some properties."

Mama Beth made eye contact. "Can I speak with you just a moment before you go?"

Did these people not realize her stretched-to-the-max schedule? "Certainly. Go get your things together, Ashton. I'll be inside in a second."

"I'll help." Carter winked at Ashton and elicited a contagious giggle from the little girl. The two headed inside where Dani still cared for the bed babies.

Concern hovered in Mama Beth's blue eyes as she laced her fingers in front of her. "I don't mean to make you worry, Mara, but I'm a little concerned about Ashton."

Mara's heart stopped momentarily, then resumed beating at a quicker pace. "Why?"

"She's just been so tired when she gets off the school bus. Today she curled up in a corner and went to sleep, even with the other children playing and making noise."

Mara kept a straight face. "Kindergarten's a big change for her. I'm sure that's all it is."

"Well, you'd be the one to know." The woman didn't sound convinced. "I just wanted to make you aware."

"Thank you." Mara laid a hand on Mama Beth's arm. "I appreciate you looking after her so well. I'll definitely keep an eye on her."

This seemed to satisfy the older woman, so Mara said her good-byes and hurried inside.

Carter and Ashton stood near the front door, unaware of her approach. With her typical child-like curiosity and grown-up demeanor, Ashton cocked her head to one side and looked up at Carter. "Are you going to be my new daddy?"

"Ashton!" Mortified, Mara hurried down the hallway to her daughter's side, grabbed the heavy backpack from her arms, and took hold of her hand. "Sweetie, let's not ask people that question, okay?"

"Why not?"

Mara stepped outside to the vehicle, then opened the back door for Ashton to crawl in. "Because it's not polite or relevant." Once her daughter was securely buckled in, Mara slid into the front seat, unnervingly aware of Carter's amused gaze latched onto her every move. Without giving him the satisfaction of acknowledging his amusement, she handed the box of chicken nuggets to the back seat, started the car, and backed out of the parking lot.

The car grew more quiet and awkward with each passing moment. And even worse, it was becoming all-too-apparent that she was hopelessly lost. On today, of all days. Had she missed a turn?

"Where is this place anyway?" Carter whispered the words, almost as though afraid of igniting her already-short and frazzled fuse.

Mara yanked the steering wheel sharply to the right, careened the car off into the grass at an intersection in the middle of nowhere, threw the gear shift into park, and reached for her county map. How could she have been so stupid not to get the location firmly fixed in her mind before bringing a client? "I think we're on the right road. And why are you whispering anyway?" The words belted out of her mouth as she slid her right index finger across the map to locate the road she needed.

"Ashton's asleep." His voice still in whisper mode, he jerked his head and left thumb toward the back seat.

She pulled down the rear view mirror. Sure enough, Ashton's head lolled to one side, eyes closed, the unopened box of chicken nuggets clutched in her hands.

Alarms rang in Mara's head and heart, but she quickly pounded them into submissive silence. Nothing to be overly-concerned about at this point. She sent a weak smile Carter's way. "Must've had a busy day at school. Probably just missed her nap." Without waiting for his response, she turned her attention back to the map.

"What road are you looking for? Maybe I can help."

Mara checked the folder for the address. "Um...County Road 2142."

A cheeky grin appeared on his face. "Other side of town." He pointed to the map. "We should've turned left instead of right."

Ugh. Fifteen minutes in the wrong direction? Mara semi-folded the map and tossed it to the floorboard. "Sorry. I'm still learning these back roads." She adjusted the rearview mirror to check for traffic, put the car in gear, and whipped around to drive the other direction, still battling panic at the sight of her sleeping daughter's paler-than-normal face.

"No prob. Maps can be confusing." Carter's sincere tone calmed her frayed nerves.

Twenty quiet minutes later, they drove onto a dirt driveway of a small rock house. A quick glance in the mirror confirmed what Mara expected.

Ashton was still asleep.

Now what should she do? "Um, I can let you in the front door to look at the place while I stay outside with her."

A frown pulled his dark brows together. "Why don't you just let me carry her? I don't mind."

Mara nodded her okay and moved to the back door to release Ashton's seat belt. Carter leaned in from the other side, his broad shoulders filling the doorway. He easily lifted her little girl from the seat. Ashton stirred momentarily, then rested her head on Carter's thick shoulders, her strawberry blond waves bright against his dark shirt.

Mara swallowed back a sudden onslaught of emotions and hurried up the front porch. Thankfully the lock box cooperated, and in a minute's time they entered the house, soft snores sounding from Ashton. The living room, though large, smelled of dust from months of disuse. Mara wrinkled her nose. "A little smelly."

"Just needs to be aired out." Carter's dark eyes scanned the space as he carefully cradled her daughter in his arms. "Really hadn't thought about a house in the country, but I like the space. And the peace and quiet."

"If your daughter drives, it would mean extra gas money each month." She clasped her hands in front of the electric blue business skirt she'd donned early that morning. The one she couldn't wait to exchange for a pair of sweat pants.

He nodded. "Good point. But let's go ahead and check out the rest of the house while we're here."

"Of course." Mara hurried him through the rest of the house, discreetly checking her watch as they entered the last bedroom. "You could use this for guests or a home office."

"You need to be somewhere?"

Man, nothing escaped this guy. He must have eyes in the back of his head. "We have an event this evening, but business comes first." She injected a happy sing-song to her words.

Carter's jaw clenched and pulsed. "Uh, no. Your family comes first."

"I know that, but this is more important than what we have scheduled for this evening." Sort of.

Without another word, and with disapproval oozing from his face, Carter strode from the room and down the hallway toward the front door, the old floors squeaking beneath his weight.

Questions rolled in her mind, but Mara followed and quickly locked up the house as she glanced over her shoulder toward the SUV.

With a soft tenderness Mara hadn't expected from this over-sized, always-aware mixture of handsome jock and caveman, Carter gently set Ashton into the seat and secured her seat belt.

Unwanted feelings unleashed inside, wreaking havoc with her stretched-out nerves. In many ways, Carter was exactly the kind of man Mara would've wished as a daddy to her little girl. Not that it mattered. Life had proved that road a dead-end.

The trip back into Miller's Creek was even more quiet than the trip out, this time with the added burden of Carter's obvious disapproval sucking the oxygen from the vehicle. Anxiety-ridden thoughts pelted Mara's brain, not just about Ashton, but about Carter Callahan. Had she somehow offended him?

www.ingramcontent.com/pod-product-compliance
Lightning Source LLC
Chambersburg PA
CBHW022129170626
46808CB00002B/907